THE LEGACY

THE WITCHES OF GREENE COUNTY

Kimberly Tobin

WHAT PEOPLE ARE SAYING

"The Legacy, Witches of Greene County **is such a fun and enlightening read, I didn't want it to end! Kimberly Tobin has woven real magical practices into a compelling story of a gifted family.**"
~Lynde Thames, Energy Healer

"A great read about family secrets, relationships and the discovery of spirituality within the self."
~Aeriol Ascher, Empowerment Leader

"A compelling fictional tale of a family who possess spiritual healing gifts and the birthright of their souls."
~Sheryl I. Glick
Author of A New Life Awaits: Spirit Guided Insights to Support Global Awakening

"If you dig books with rich characters, a little bit of woo and a sprinkle of wry humor, check this one out. I think you'll like it."
~Lisa Wechtenhiser
Intuitive Guide, Coach, Teacher and All-Around Groovy Chick

The Legacy:

The Witches of Greene County

Copyright © 2020 by Kimberly Tobin

RHG Media Productions
25495 Southwick Drive #103
Hayward, CA 94544.

ISBN 9781735687704

Visit us on line at www.YourPurposeDrivenPractice.com

Printed in the United States of America.

ACKNOWLEDGMENTS

To Tim, for always being the rock so that I could fly; to Adam and Addison for loving me in all my weirdness; to Dad, who's support gives me the strength to be truly me; to Lynde for being my soul sister on this amazing ride. I would not have been able to experience this amazing life without any of you.

CHAPTER 1

MINA

It was a beautiful day in the upper Midwest, unusual for this time of year. Mina could feel the sun on her face as she walked through the park. As she approached a bench, she decided to sit and soak in the warm, bright sun. This small decision was a big deal. It wasn't that long ago that she wasn't allowed to make any decisions or if she did she would face the consequences of them being wrong. Mina would never take her freedom of choice for granted again.

As Mina sat on the bench feeling the warmth on her face, her mind drifted. Suddenly she could taste the warm blood from her busted lip. Her eye was throbbing as it continued to swell. Her ribs stabbed her with every small breath she tried to take.

"Don't open your eyes, don't move a muscle. Just play dead and hopefully this time he will leave you alone." Mina kept telling herself over and over.

He, Brock, had just beaten her up again. How did this happen? Mina didn't wake up one day and decide she wanted to be in an abusive relationship. Hell, she tried her best to stay out of relationships because they were always just too much drama. But then she met Brock and he swept her off her feet. He was a very handsome and fun loving guy; the life of the party. He had so many friends (or so it seemed) as everywhere they went, everyone knew Brock. He could tell the best jokes, make everyone laugh and have a great time. The first few weeks they were together, life was a party! Mina d actually let her guard down and started dreaming about happily ever after.

Brock had stayed at her house one night and just never left. That was fine with Mina. It felt so natural. They seemed to go out almost every night at first. She usually met him at the bar after work for a drink that turned into a few drinks then stumbling home.

After a month or so, this lifestyle was wreaking havoc on Mina's body, mind and work. All that alcohol, lack of sleep and poor diet was extremely hard on her stomach and she was having a hard time keeping anything down. She was sick, exhausted and not thinking clearly at work. She had mentioned to Brock that she wanted to stay home one night, fix him a nice dinner instead of going out. This way Mina could show off her cooking skills, to get to know Brock more personally and she hoped to start on that path of happily ever after.

That was the first time he hit her. And it wasn't the last. The beatings became more frequent and more severe. Of course he was sorry each time, promising he'd never do it again. Don't think she didn't try to break up with him, but he kept coming to her house. He made all kinds of threats if she called the police or told anyone anything. Besides, no one would believe a tramp like her, according to him. Just look how many friends he had and how much everyone loved him!

It had been over six months that she had endured his abuse. And today, as she swallowed the blood from her busted lip, she knew this was the last time. She was done being beaten and raped because she deserved it, so he said. Mina lay there quietly, but in her head she was begging God to give her strength, to please send angels to guide her and protect her as she figured out a way to end this nightmare. Isn't that what her grandmother had taught her?

"Prayer work in good times and bad" Mina swore she could hear her Grandmother whisper that phrase in her ear.

Mina hadn't done her prayer work in a very long time but at that very moment she silently promised to continue no matter what.

Mina heard Brock slam the door, start his car and pull out of the driveway. This was her chance and she took it! She pulled her battered body off the floor chanting to herself over and over again "prayer work makes the dream work". Mina packed the things that meant the most to her and stuffed them in her SUV. She wrote Brock's name on a piece of paper and flushed it down the toilet. Then she called one of those companies that buy houses as is and met with them that day. Mina took the offer, gave the agent an address to her grandmother's house to mail the check, and headed out of town towards her new, safe life.

As Mina sat on the park bench, she smiled to herself realizing that this was the first day she had actually done her prayer work, as well as, anything magical without her grandmother by her side. Mina had actually create the miracle she so desired – no more Brock.

CHAPTER 2

Mina got up from the park bench and continued her stroll. She was ready, ready for something big. Yes, what she had done to get where she was at this moment had been a bunch of little steps that culminated to something big. Now that she felt like she was on solid ground, safe, she had the yearning for something more.

Mina had experienced many miracles since the day she moved to the city. The flushing spell was the first of many rituals she had done to create those miracles. When she needed a parking spot close to the store, she simply asked her angels for the perfect spot. Every single time that she remembered to ask, there as a parking spot available for her. If money was tight, she would do a quick rhyme, shake quarters in a jar and within twenty-four hours, extra money would show up. Mina didn't consider her Prayer Work magical, however, daily Mina found herself receiving guidance more and more.

Mina knew deep down that this was only the tip of the iceberg. Her faith in God and the Universe had grown so much over the past several months. She could see that by asking for the little things like parking place, synchronicities would show up. It's not like she heard a deep voice telling her to take a left instead of a right. Mina just had feelings. For instance, if she had asked to arrive at a particular place safely and quickly, she would ask "left or right" at the stop sign. When she said "left" she would feel butterflies in her stomach versus when she said "right" she either felt nothing or heaviness. Mina was getting much better at following these feelings. Some would say she just simply had a hunch but when Mina did follow the feelings, she would arrive faster than she expected and safely. When she didn't, she was always late from being stuck behind a school bus or a traffic jam.

Still, to Mina this was all small stuff. Oh, she loved the feeling of knowing that her angels and guides were with her at every moment. Mina never felt alone, yet this yearning for something deeper was keeping her awake at night. On one of those sleepless nights, she grabbed her tablet and started mindlessly scrolling social media. A post for a group "The Mystics Path" grabbed her attention. She found herself reading multiple posts from this group. Mina resonated with each one. These people were or had felt the same things she was! She wasn't going crazy!

The group participants who had posted seemed to have similar beliefs in God, goddesses, angels and guides. They were somewhere a bit more out there than Mina currently was but she was open to their points of view. She knew she didn't know everything and what better place to learn than from a group of people who had the same core beliefs and thoughts? Mina instantly felt at a connection to the group and she read post after post after post until she could no longer keep her eyes open. She fell asleep with a deep sense of belonging and connection, something she had yet to find in her new location.

CHAPTER 3

Since Mina had been in the city, she had been working at a small company as an office manager. This was new to Mina, not the office part but the office manager role. She couldn't help but appreciate Jennifer, her old office manager, more and more each day. In her old life Mina was a CPA along with two others in the company. Mina always assumed that she and the others ran the office but after having the role of office manager, she knew that Jennifer was the key to the firm's success.

Mina took the position of an administrator almost a year after she had come to the city so that she could go to work for eight hours a day and leave the job at the office each night. She was determined to find balance between work and life. Mostly, she was adamant to find herself. Mina was really good at burying herself in her work allowing her to be the good fixer she was raised to be. Hard work was the only way to get ahead in life according to her family.

With her increasing knowledge of her faith, Mina found herself yearning to incorporate her faith in every single area of her life, including work. Mina promised herself that she would do at least one spiritual thing every single day. It wasn't as if she donned a big black cloak and strutted into the office or the grocery store. It wasn't like she stood on a street corning yelling about her beliefs. It was small things like stirring her coffee clockwise while whispering her intentions for the day; or asking her angels for help when she was stuck in traffic. Mina was getting really good at the day to day rituals. And each night, she loved journaling about how the day had progressed. Still, there was something deeper that kept calling Mina.

As Mina sat with her journal one night, she asked herself "What else is possible?" She knew that her life was solid from the outside looking in. She had a good job, no real worries about money, a small townhouse and some acquaintances at work. But that damn yearning for more would not leave her. Mina asked herself "What is it that I really want to do?" Of course she came up instantly with the pat answers she had learned to have: work hard and make loads of money. She knew that wasn't the real answer for her so she asked herself again: "What is it that I really want to do?" Mina could not answer that question before she fell asleep, journal and pen still in her hands.

After a restless night of tossing and turning, Mina woke with that same question on her mind: "What is it I really want to do?" She kept coming up with things that she didn't want to do, like; work eighty hours a week for just a paycheck; work so that someone else profited from her long hours; save big corporations without faces. Even though it seemed like Mina was not making much ground in search of what she wanted to do, figuring out what she didn't want was just as important. At least this gave her some frame-work, and so she kept asking herself this same question for days.

CHAPTER 4

While on her tablet one night, her favorite social media page had mentioned a metaphysical store a few miles from her apartment. Mina found herself both intrigued and skeptical. She believed that those stores were only for devil worshipers and that only weird, crazy people who killed cats for their blood spells frequented them. And, yet, the members in her social media group were nothing like that. Mina had come to learn that spells were just prayers to a higher power and every religion had them.

Mina found herself scrolling the store's website. It didn't mention anything about blood spells or killing animals. She laughed out loud. The website was full of information and listed some classes that everyone was welcomed. Mina clicked off her tablet with the intention of visiting the store on Saturday.

Saturday morning Mina found herself up an hour earlier than normal. She was almost giddy with excitement about going to the metaphysical store. She also found herself very apprehensive and honestly scared. What would she find? Were there really animal blood collecting kits? Would they place a spell on her so that she wouldn't be able to leave the store? Would they make her join a cult? "Okay Mina, get a grip! You know this fear isn't yours. Return to sender!" Instantly, Mina felt the fear leave.

Finally it was time to leave for the store. The anticipation was killing her. Her stomach was in knots and felt like a million butterflies were flying around in there. Mina asked her angels for confirmation "Okay guys, if I'm supposed to go to this store, show me a sign on the way and have a parking place in the front row available for me! And thank you!"

Mina started her car and headed towards the store.

While driving to her destination, Mina was lost in thought. That same question of "What do I really want to do?" still stuck in her mind. She knew she wanted to help people and deal with them one on one, not faceless corporations. Yet, she wasn't sure what she could help them with. Deep in thought, Mina almost missed the billboard that said "Angel On My Shoulder" as an advertisement for some piece of jewelry.

"Thanks guys! I got that! I'm glad you are with me!"

As Mina pulled into the store parking lot, of course there was a spot right in front of the store.

She actually expected nothing less. She knew it was just for her as she saw two other cars drive right past the open spot and pull into empty ones farther away.

"Thank you! I saw that too!" Mina gets out of her car and can feel her breath quicken.

"What in the hell is up with me?" she thought.

She stopped for a moment and leaned against her car. Was this fear she was feeling or excitement? Mina remembered that fear and excitement feel the same way in one's body. When she asked herself again "Is this fear?" she got a heavy feeling. So she asked, "Is this excitement?" and the butterflies went wild. Mina knew without a doubt she was in the right place. She took a deep breath and walked in the store.

The first thing Mina noticed was the smell, a sweet and calming scent. Mina wasn't sure if it was the smell or the energy, but she felt instantly at ease.

"Good morning. Is there anything I can help you find?" the store clerk asked her.

Mina felt herself blush because she was surprised that the clerk looked so normal. "Good Morning. I'm just looking for now."

"Great. If there is anything I can help you find or if you have any questions, my name is Savannah, and that's Ellie over there. We are happy to assist you with anything."

"Thank you so much" replied Mina.

Mina continued to soak in every single inch of that store. She didn't even realize that she had placed so many items in her basket. There were candles and incense, a clear quartz crystal and a rose quartz crystal, a couple of books, and a beautiful new deck of tarot cards with angels on them. She found herself at the announcement board where there was a list of the upcoming classes being held at the store. Each one of the classes intrigued her more than the last one.

After about what seemed like fifteen minutes, Mina headed to the register to check out.

Savannah asked her if she found everything she was looking for.

Mina laughed and said, "I don't think I can fit any more items in the basket!"

"Oh, I can definitely get you another basket and help you to your car if you like." laughed Savannah.

Ellie was also behind the counter and extended a hand introducing herself. "Hi, I'm Ellie. Savannah and I own the shop. We are glad you stopped by. You don't look familiar, is this your first time here?"

Mina answered "Nice to meet you. I'm Mina. And yes, this is the first time I've had the pleasure of stopping in. But it won't be my last!"

"Yay!" replied Savannah. "We love our customers - new and regulars. What do you do Mina?"

"I'm an office manager here in town."

Ellie and Savannah looked at each other trying to be inconspicuous.

"Ask her," whispered Savanna to Ellie. "Ask her."

Ellie shook her head. Mina asked instead "Ask me what?" Ellie looked around and realized that there was no one else in the store so she thought, "What the hell, it can't hurt". Ellie replied, "You see, Savannah and I own and run this store and we pride ourselves in offering only high energy items. Yet, we are terrible at keeping the books so we have been setting our intentions and doing what we can to call in someone that could possibly help us."

"When you walked into the store, I just had a knowing about you" Savannah piped in.

"Stop Savannah! Ms. Mina is not here to help us. She's here to gather things for herself."

"What kind of things do you need help with?"

asked Mina. "Actually, in my old life, I was a CPA and I still have my certifications."

"A CPA? And you are working as an office manager?" asked Ellie.

"Long story" smiled Mina and Ellie gave her that knowing nod.

Ellie cringed, "We can't afford a CPA, but thank you."

Mina asked how she would know because she hadn't even said anything about her rates. Ellie smiled and Savannah just stood there clapping her hands quietly.

Mina asked, "How about I trade you in helping with the accounting for taking one of your classes?"

Ellie's eyes got big, and she replied, "You'd do that?"

"Hell yeah," replied Mina.

Savannah stuck out her hand and said, "You got a deal!" motioning with her head for Ellie to do the same.

All smiling, the three agreed on the new arrangements. Mina gave the girls her number and said she would get in touch with them next week. Ellie told Mina she was all signed up for the next class and would see her soon. Mina left with her new treasures which included a new friendship.

CHAPTER 5

On Wednesday afternoon, the courier stopped by the office with a letter. This wasn't anything unusual for the office; in fact, it was almost a daily thing. What was unusual is that this time the certified letter was for Mina. She signed for the letter as her heart sank into her stomach. What in the world could this be? She really didn't think anyone knew where she was, let alone where she worked. This could not be good.

Slowly Mina opened the envelope and took out a letter. As she unfolded the note she realized the letter was from Sheila the She-Devil, or in other words, Mom. Mina realized that most people don't call their mothers by their first name, let alone a She-Devil, but Sheila was not the epitome of motherhood. Growing up, Mina used to swear that woman was a secret agent or something. In her little girl mind, there was no other reason a person could be so cold and mean. To say that Mina never felt good enough as her child was an understatement.

Oh, hell! Sheila was coming for a visit in three days. Dammit! Not only did Mina not want to deal with Sheila, she didn't want to miss her class with Ellie. She knew that this class on intuition was very important. Even though she wasn't sure exactly why, Mina knew she couldn't miss it. She would just have to call Sheila later and change the dates. As Mina rolled her eyes knowing that nothing ever changed Sheila's mind or plans, she put the letter in her purse and went back to her work.

Mina took a long walk after work dreading the connection with her mother. Why was there such a disconnect with Sheila? Where were the warm fuzzies a little girl got from her mom? Mina could not remember one time when Sheila ever made her feel secure and loved. She couldn't even think of an instance that her mom had given her a warm, caring hug. Warmth was definitely not Sheila's strong point.

With phone in hand, Mina took a deep breath and pressed the call button.

"Sheila Jacobson."

"Hello Mother" Mina said, wondering why in the hell her mom answered the phone that way knowing the caller ID said it was Mina calling.

"Hello, Mina. I'm assuming you got my note as I can think of no other reason you would call. You haven't called in months."

"Yes, Mother, I did get your note today. I was definitely shocked to see that you were coming here in three days. Is it a work thing?"

"Of course it's a work thing. You know my job takes me all over the world. And I just thought I would take a few extra days and spend some time with you."

Mina's heart was in her stomach again knowing that since it was a work thing there would be no flexibility with the schedule.

"I'll be staying with you since you have the room. You do have an extra bedroom, right?"

Mina found herself contemplating stretching the truth and telling her mother that she only had a one bedroom apartment but knowing that Sheila would see it, she had to tell her the truth. "Yes, Mother, I have a spare bedroom for you to stay in, with your own bathroom." Mina said before her judgmental mother could ask.

"Great! I will see you Saturday morning nine am sharp" Sheila responded.

"Mother, I absolutely have to work on Saturday

morning. I am meeting with a client for a few hours. I can meet you for lunch and we can go to my house after that."

It wasn't a complete lie. Ellie and Savannah were her new clients.

"Fine," said Sheila "I'll meet you Saturday noon at Monte's" and hung up.

"Of course," thought Mina, "the only four-star place within thirty miles

Mina looked at her phone as the call disconnected. There, again, no warm fuzzies, no "I love you," no "I can't wait to see you." Nothing. She felt like she was just another client to her mother. But what kind of client it was, Mina actually had no idea because she had no idea what her mother did as a profession. Sheila called herself a consultant, but Mina honestly could not tell you what her mother consulted. Maybe Sheila really was a spy, Mina chuckled as she put the phone on the counter and went about her evening. At least she had a "suitable to Sheila" excuse for being unavailable during the class time.

CHAPTER 6

Finally it was Saturday. Mina thought this day would never get here. She was up at 4:00 a.m., filled with excitement and anticipation for the class at the bookstore. As she walked through her home she could almost forget that Sheila was coming today. Almost. Mina focused her energy and good thoughts back to the class as she went from room to room making sure every single thing was in its place and clean. She laughed to herself as she had an imagine of Sheila walking around with white gloves on checking for dust in every corner and finding salt that Mina had blessed the house with.

Mina was dressed and ready to leave two hours before the class was to start. Her excuse to herself was that this would give her time to speak with Ellie and Savannah about the accounting work they needed her to do, but in reality, she just couldn't wait any longer to get to that store. On her way, she remembered to ask the angels for a close parking place and a safe trip.

Then she heard a soothing angelic voice say "Remember."

On one had it kind of startled Mina and on the other hand it was comforting and familiar. "Remember?" asked Mina, "Remember what?" Did she forget to turn off her hair straightener? Did she forget to lock the door? Mina could visually see herself turning off the flat iron and locking the door. What in the hell was she supposed to remember? As Mina pulled into the parking lot to the open spot at the front, she completely forgot about the angelic message. She was just too damn excited about being at that store.

"Good morning ladies" Mina waved as she walked in.

"Hi!" said Savannah with a great big smile. She seem to really like Mina and her energy, Ellie looked at her watch, appearing to be thinking she must be running really behind then, felt relief as realized it was Mina who was extremely early.

"Hello Mina. You're awfully early for class. Did you need help finding something?"

"I'm not here just for the class. I'm hoping we could get started on looking over the books so that I could start paying off my debt" Mina said with a grin.

The store was usually pretty quiet early on Saturday mornings so Ellie motioned for her to come to the back room so they could get going. As she came closer and Ellie put her arm over Mina's shoulder, Ellie got a message for Mina: "Just remember."

Ellie said "Okay, got it."

"Got what?" Mina asked.

"Just a quick message. I'll tell you about it later when the time is right."

Mina shrugged and they continued to the back room.

At the desk, Mina almost laughed at the sight. There were papers everywhere; unopened mail, bills from every month of the year, some paid, some not, inventory, broken candles and gum. The only thing missing was an empty space. Ellie tried to shove stuff into piles but she didn't even know what she was piling up.

Mina gently took her hand and said "It's okay. I've got this. No judgment here, just help. We'll get through this together and in a very short time we'll know exactly where to focus and make changes if necessary." Mina knew that this was Ellie's baby, her life, her mission and Mina would handle it with love and care. Probably more gently than any other client she had ever had. Mina loved this place, the people, the books, the jewelry, all of it, and she was going to do everything she could to help them succeed.

Ellie's shoulders relaxed knowing it was in good hands, hands she trusted. That trust thing was very difficult when it came to people and her store. Savannah was adopted into the family when Ellie had to miss work, but she was the only one Ellie let this close. Until Mina.

Mina started putting things into piles: broken candles and torn books in one area, paid bills in another. Soon she had everything down to six piles. There was even an empty space on the desk where she could start writing in her notebook. Mina called for Ellie to come to the back room so they could start going over things as she wanted to see if she could take a stack or two home with her to continue to work on.

As Ellie came to the door her eyes lit up with astonishment. "Damn, Girl, that was fast! And it's so neat!"

"In this pile are the paid invoices and in this pile are the unpaid invoices. I was wondering if I could take these two piles and the inventory list home so that I could dive into them in more details," Mina asked.

Ellie felt like someone was pulling a vein out of her heart. She looked at her watch and said, "We need to get to going, class is about to start!"

Mina could not believe how fast the time had flown while she was working on the piles. Usually when she was doing the beginning stages of account review, time would drag because she hated this part. But not this time; it felt like only a few minutes had passed. Mina quickly grabbed her stuff and headed to the classroom as Ellie grabbed her heart in relief for avoiding an answer to Mina's question of taking a part of her life out of the store.

Mina sat at a long table with her notebook and pen neatly in front of her. She was ready for this class. Hell, she had been counting down the minutes since she saw it on the bulletin board. She was ready to take a million notes, writing every single word Ellie said to the class. There were five others in the room besides the teacher and Mina, but she didn't notice anyone else because she was so focused on what was about to happen.

Ellie could feel the apprehension in the room so she had everyone scoot back from the tables, place their hands on their laps, palms up, and take three deep breathes with her, in through the nose and out through the mouth. Once the energy felt more relaxed, Ellie allowed everyone to move back up to the tables.

"This first class will allow you each to get a feel on how I receive the messages from Spirit. Trust that everyone does it differently, you will do it differently. I'm here to give you guidelines on how to ready yourself to receive the messages from Spirit."

Ellie walked around the table and continued. "For example, I hear words and I see pictures, sometimes an entire story. Others will get feelings and some just know without knowing how they know. There are people that see, know, hear, smell and feel." She again paused to let the information sink in for her students.

"The point is to trust that your way of receiving the messages is the perfect way for you. Sounds simple, right? Actually it is. It's like a muscle; the more you use it the easier and strong it gets. The problem? FEAR. We let ourselves talk us out of the possibility that Spirit is talking to us. 'I'm not good enough for that.' 'That answer was just too easy it couldn't be from God.' Does anyone remember the burning bush from the Bible?"

All of her students shook their heads yes in a quiet response. "There are tons of ways that Spirit communicates with us. I'm going to give you the safe space to explore the ways that you have experienced and will experience this communication. Some call it intuition and some call it psychic abilities. Whatever you call it, that sense is your birth right."

Ellie looked above their heads and heard "Remember." Ellie smiled and said, "Thanks for that" and everyone knew she was talking to her angels or guides or God or whomever, but not them.

Ellie continued "I'm here to help you remember your gifts, flex that muscle and start using the guidance in your every-day life."

Mina sat straight up in her chair "Remember" she heard again. She knew she was in the right place at the right time.

CHAPTER 7

As she left the classroom, Mina's mind was spinning with all the new information she had just been presented. It was as if she couldn't form a complete sentence in her mind and yet things had started to make sense. Hunches, prayers, angels, guides, God, Spirit, intuition, imagination, seeing and knowing things that others hadn't, all stuff she had written off as being tired or stressed. Mina started her car and just sat there trying to come back to Earth with her thoughts; she did have to meet with the She-Devil soon. Putting the car in drive, Mina quickly did her "snow globe" prayer in preparation of the meeting with her mother. She imagined a ball of energy around herself and Sheila, pulling in words for the intentions of the meeting: calm, loving, peaceful, easy and short. Once the energy felt complete, Mina released the ball of energy that contained the intentions to her angels. Mina called this a snow globe prayer because the words floating in the ball of energy surrounding the subject looked like a snow globe to her.

Before Mina realized it, she was in front of Monte's where a perfect parking spot was waiting just for her.

"Thanks guys! I didn't even remember to ask for this one" she said to her angels as she parked.

As she stepped up to the hostess station a polite young girl greeted her "Good afternoon. You must be Ms. Mina. We've been expecting you. This way please."

Mina wasn't even sure if she had acknowledged that she was who they were expecting and found herself wondering how in the world they knew who she was as she followed the hostess to the back of the restaurant where her mother was sitting.

"Hello, Mother"

"Hello, dear. You look good"

"Thank you, Mother. Mina replied as she felt her armor go up around her, ready for Sheila's impending judgment on everything Mina said, did, wore, ordered and even how she breathed, "You look beautiful as always, Mother".

Both ladies ordered and made small talk all through the light lunch. Mina's "spidey" senses were on high alert and she could swear something was going on with Sheila. Maybe it was just the class this morning that had her mind going, creating all different kind of scenarios to explain the reason for the out-of-the-blue visit. However, there was no explaining away the overall energy of Sheila. Was she just tired, did she have some big secret mission that was going wrong, was she dying? Whatever the reason, Mina knew something just wasn't right. As the two were leaving the beautiful establishment and getting into Mina's car, she found herself hoping that Sheila would open up more once they got to her home.

The drive was pretty quiet for the most part. Sheila was taking in the surroundings, not as something she hadn't seen before, but with a familiar appreciation for the historic buildings that were now occupied by businesses, townhouses, and apartments. Yes, Sheila had been here many times, mentally and physically. She loved this part of the city. It was like each brick and stone spoke to her, the trees waved and greeted her like a long lost friend. In her mind, she lovingly waved and sent energetic hugs to them all. She also asked for all of their help.

Thank you all for the love you are sending me. Please also surround Mina with your love and light. I'm not sure how's she going to take this information but I know in my soul it's time to tell her.

"I'm sorry, Mother; I didn't hear what you said. Could you please repeat that?"

"Well shit," thought Sheila. She hadn't realized that Mina had honed her skills in telepathy. Sheila was going to have to be way more careful of her thoughts and communications. "I didn't say anything, honey. I was holding in a sneeze."

"Are you sick, Mom?"

"Oh, no, not at all. Probably just allergies or something. I'm good" Sheila replied.

They both knew that was a lie. Thankfully, they were at Mina's house so their attention was pointed in a different direction. They both got out of the car and headed to the front door. Mina found it a bit odd that Sheila walked right up to her door. How did she know which home was hers? Mina was extremely careful not to put anything personal out front. Yes, in the back of her mind, she was still hiding from Brock.

"Here, Mother, let me unlock the door and show you around." Mina gave her that questioning look and it reminded Sheila that she had to be more careful to act like this was the first time she had seen this home.

Sheila consciously sent loving energy to the home and surrounded Mina with love and light. She knew the next few hours and days could be rough for Mina, for them both. Sheila had to share her world with Mina. It was time to be truthful - well, as truthful as she could. Sheila knew that Mina thought she was a spy. It was safer for her to just believe that and it wasn't a total lie. It was a good cover that explained the detachment from her daughter, her only child, her life. She hoped that Mina could understand and forgive Sheila for distance. Sheila's mother had done the same thing to her. But she got to be the good grandmother while Sheila had to be the absent mother. It had been that was for many generations.

After Mina had shown her home to her mom and had taken her bags to her room, Mina offered, "Mother, would you like some tea or a glass of wine?"

"Oh, hot tea sounds amazing. Thank you."

Mina put the water on and readied a serving tray to bring to the living room. Mina loved her tea pot. Her grandmother had passed it down to her. One of the great memories she had of her grandma was them sharing late afternoon tea. Grandma always had the best varieties of flavored tea and honey. Sometimes they would sit in silence, and sometimes they would talk about random things like the garden, the moon or the trees. Mina cherished her grandmother and wondered how her own mother could be so very different.

Mina brought the tray into the living room where her mother seemed to be pacing.

"Okay, Mom. What's up? Something is bothering you. Are you sick? Did you lose your job? Do you need money? Please tell me. You are starting to really worry me."

Trying to dodge the question, Sheila said "So, tell me about this new class you are taking."

Mina's eyes got so big and her heart sank to her stomach. Here it goes, the judgment, the tongue thrashing for embarrassing the family even though she's hundreds of miles away from them. And, how in the hell did she know about it? Was Ellie a spy too? Or was Savannah a big ass tattle tale?

"I know you are wondering how I know about this class. I haven't been spying on you. But I do know things about you that you think no one else could know. I have things that I need to share with you. It's big and it will change your world - well, your perception of it anyway."

Mina felt like she was having a heart attack. Her chest was crushing, she couldn't breathe, and she was so dizzy. All of the sudden, she could see her mom forming a big white ball of energy and shooting it towards her. Her heart calmed down, she could breathe and everything seemed so bright. Mina and Sheila were in this ball of loving, protective energy. Mina looked around and could see that her whole house was encompassed in this energy. Many times Mina had sent a ball of energy to others but never included herself so she didn't realize what it actually felt or looked like.

"I know, I have a lot of explaining to do. That's why I'm here. I'll answer any questions you have and tell you what I feel you can handle. I'll explain to you how Grandma explained to me, and her mom explained to her. Stop me at any time with questions. Deal?"

Mina could barely shake her head in response. She tried to pick up the cup of tea but when she looked at the beloved tea pot it hit her like a ton of bricks that her grandmother was in on this, too. Whatever the hell "this" was.

As Mina sat in this ball of protective, loving of energy with her mother, she kept thinking that she should be way more upset about this than she was feeling. But she felt so calm and open. It reminded her of when Brock left for the last time. She knew she had to do something, so she did it - no fear, just calm.

"Ok Mother. Let's have it."

CHAPTER 8

Sheila began with a sincere apology. "Mina, first I want you to know that I hated every minute I was away from you. I knew the feeling of not having your mother by your side growing up and I swore when I had a daughter, the last thing I would do was to abandon her like my mom had. I, too, was raised by my grandmother. I swore my mom was some kind of spy. Don't get me wrong, I loved Grammy, but grew up thinking my mom didn't like being around me and dropped me off for someone else to raise. I didn't fit in at school, had no friends except Grammy and felt so very alone for so long." Sheila paused, feeling the loneliness again and hurting for doing the same to Mina. "I promise that I knew every laugh, scrape, and cry you had because I checked in every single day see how you were."

"I just don't understand, Mother. If you knew how I felt why did you stay away? Why did you let Meme raise me?" Mina was having a hard time with the story that her Meme had been an absent mother. Meme was so good to Mina growing up.

She taught her things like gardening: when to plant, talking to those plants as they grew and appreciating the fruits as they canned each summer. Meme was a natural with animals and birds. Mina could remember thinking that each song a bird sang felt as if it was specifically for Meme. Stray cats and dogs weren't strays for long as each found love, care and food at Meme's house. And, cooking! That woman could cook plain green beans and have them taste better than any meal at a five star restaurant, including Monte's. How could this be the same woman who abandoned Sheila?

"Are you a spy?"

"I'm not a spy working for a government agency, if that's what you're asking me. I am, we are called in the old country, a Curandero. Some call us witches, psychics, medicine women, or shamans. Many generations ago our ancestors were the only doctors in the towns. Through the decades the roles have changed a bit, but we are still sought after for our abilities."

Mina's head was spinning listening to Sheila unfold this story. Mina felt like she had a devil on one shoulder and an angel on the other fighting back and forth. Her mind was telling her that this was a big ass lie and yet her soul was connecting the dots and making sense of so many questions she had as a little girl.

"This is just too far-fetched" her mind screamed and yet, on the other had Mina felt lighter than ever before. "Okay, Mom, I need a break. This is just too much to soak in at this moment."

"Oh, I get it, honey. Please, ask me anything" Sheila said as she opened her arms walking towards Mina. Mina turned to go to her room, Sheila replied "whenever you are ready" as the door slammed.

CHAPTER 9

Mina lay on her bed with her mind going in a thousand different directions. She somehow felt betrayed by her entire lineage. She felt angry for being lied to by Meme and Sheila and yet felt empathy for Sheila. In this modern age, how could there be such a need for witches? There was a Doc-in-the-Box on every single corner and at least two big hospitals in every city. In the next second Mina realized she had felt that doctors seemed to treat symptoms and not the core issues and that Meme had taught her many natural remedies for things like headaches, insomnia and cramps. Ugh! She was so confused.

Mina got out of her bed and headed to the living room, but Sheila wasn't there. An instant panic rose from her heart and she caught her breath. "She can't be gone!" Mina thought and finally she let out her breath as she saw her mom standing on the deck. Wow, that reaction surprised the hell out of Mina.

Mina walked quietly through the French doors and stood by her mom. Neither said a word, not even to acknowledge the other's presence. Mina could feel the cool, night air on her face. She then could imagine a breeze going through her head, clearing all the fog and confusion of the day. She then felt the energy go through her throat, through her chest and stomach, easing all the tension Mina had been holding onto for so long. Mina could see in her imagination the breeze going through every cell and molecule in her body, everywhere except her lower belly. Meme had taught Mina when she was young about her chakras and she instantly knew that there was a block in her root chakra. Mina concentrated on that area of her body and intentionally sent white light to that area as she asked the breeze to clear her root chakra of all lower energies. After a couple of minutes, Mina could see in her mind's eye that all of her chakras had been cleansed and aligned by the breeze and white light of God's love.

"Feels good to cleanse with the breeze, doesn't it?" Sheila asked.

"Yes it does. How did you know that's what I was doing?"

"Because my grandmother taught me long ago about my chakras and how to cleanse them. I could see and feel your energy doing it exactly how I do it."

Mina's mind went into another tailspin. Was she

doing the magic all along not even knowing it was a traditional thing? Mina had grown up thinking that everyone did this all the time.

"Mina, every family and religion have their own traditions. And clearing your chakras isn't magic, it's an energy thing. Besides, what exactly do you think magic is? In your mind is it something that is bad, scary?"

In Mina's mind, magic was the devil-worshipping that all the kids used to tease her about in school. The kids were so mean and called her family devil worshipers. Meme didn't even mention the devil to Mina, ever.

"You know, Mom, I really can't answer that. Before visiting the metaphysical shop, I used to think it was kitten blood poured over a large white candle in the middle of the forest by some weirdo cloaked in black velvet telling the devil to kill someone or the devil telling them to kill someone! Honestly, I laughed to myself when I walked into that store and didn't see one dead animal or blood on any shelf. I really loved the feel of the store, the ladies and was intrigued by every single item. Some things felt so familiar and some so very interesting, I just wanted to buy everything and bring it home with me. I would probably still be there if I didn't have to meet you for lunch.

I haven't felt so comfortable or at home anywhere else in this city—other than my home."

"Oh, I understand completely, Mina. I love that store too. That Ellie is one strong woman."

Mina looked at her mother in complete surprise. It was Ellie who told her mother everything, dammit! Mina thought she could trust her.

As if Sheila was reading Mina's mind she replied, "No, Ellie didn't tattle on you. Without breaking any confidentiality, I have worked with Ellie for a few years now. She was a very sick woman and the doctors had all given up hope for her. Now she's getting healthier by the day and getting her life back on track. That store is her life and I understand you are helping her with that. It wasn't conjured up or planned. Ellie knew the minute you spoke that you were my daughter. Savannah doesn't know much so I would ask that you keep the subject to yourself."

Mina walked over and plopped into the big outdoor chair by the fire. She had the strangest feelings. All of this was almost too much to handle, yet she felt more at peace than ever before, more so than just an hour ago. It was all so foreign and yet all so familiar. As Mina stared into the fire, images of Meme teaching her about plants, animals, weather, water and so much more danced. Each flame brought a picture of something that connected deep in her soul. It was if Mina was watching a movie of her life.

Then it hit her: "So, I'm your next client?"

CHAPTER 10

"You are not my client, Mina, and you never will be. I hope you never have to understand how devastatingly hard this has been on me to not be with you. I want to make that up to you. I want to be able to help you grow into your own magic and abilities."

"Oh NO!" Mina interrupted "I'm not doing what you did or what you do. I'm not leaving my family, my children to run all over the world for others. I'm not doing it! I'm not even 'magical' or gifted. I'm an accountant, not a healer! This life is NOT for me!"

"Fortunately you get to choose. I got to choose, but I didn't honestly feel like I had a choice. Healing is my passion and my gifts allow me to pursue that passion. I'm not here to force this life of healing on you. What kind of healer would you be if you hated what you are doing? Look around, Mina, people are dying each day doing what they hate. This life can be so full of fear that it completely hides any passion one might have. Fear keeps them isolated, secluded and small. I would never force you to embark on a journey that you weren't passionate about."

"So you choose your work over me? You just dumped me off at Meme's and trotted off to God knows where for yourself?!"

Sheila hung her head and replied "that's a little harsh but true. No excuse, but what kind of mother would I be if I didn't follow my passion? I was given these gifts to help others. You were in the best hands possible with Mom. I was raised with the expectation I would follow in her footsteps no matter what. The ONLY way I agreed to take over the family business was that Mom promised that she would never ever put those expectations on you. I'm not putting those expectations on you now and won't. I want to support what you want. I want to help you follow your passions. Do you know what those are?"

Mina sat there not knowing how to respond. She heard what her mom said, and yet she was still having that internal fight of hating her and wanting to hug her. Mina was a compassionate person, knowing there were always several sides to any story. She just never considered her mom's side. And yet, Mina had really never felt the level of passion about something that she would drop off her kid for someone else to raise." Her head was spinning! Mina couldn't believe that Sheila had been here less than twelve hours! She got up to go to the kitchen asking Sheila if she would like a glass of wine, too.

"Just bring the bottle!" Sheila replied following Mina back into the kitchen.

"Mom, I don't even know what my passions are. I've been asking myself this quite a lot lately and have no answer. It's so frustrating and now on a much bigger level than yesterday."

Sheila asked, "What do you love to do?"

Mina shrugged. "I really don't know."

"So what do you hate do to?"

"How is that going to help me? I don't want to do what I hate."

"Exactly" said Sheila "when you can figure out what you don't want to do it gets you closer to what you do want to do."

"Good point, Mom. I hate working for names on paper. You know, big, faceless companies just pushing numbers around so they can make millions. I do like working with numbers, they're so definite: two plus two always equals four. And it makes me laugh to watch people who think math is hard. Like Ellie for instance. She's let her business paperwork pile up so much it's difficult for her to make heads or tails out of it. I went in there and in a short couple of hours I had everything organized. I literally can not wait to get back in there and solve that problem and help her learn to love that side of the business too." Mina's face was beaming!

"It seems to me you do know your passion."

"Oh, yeah? In that short explanation of what I hate you found my passion?" Mina asked.

"No, I didn't find your passion, it's written all over your face. You are glowing."

"What do you mean 'it seems I do know my passion'? I don't have any idea other than I hate working for big companies saving corporations' asses."

"And I see a passion for helping small business with their books!" said Sheila as she took another sip of wine.

Were they actually breaking down walls here, or was it just the wine? Sheila hoped it was the wine helping the barriers melt away.

She could see Mina's wheels spinning. "So, how do you feel about helping small businesses love their books, and in turn, make money?"

"You know, you're right Mom! Small businesses fail so often because they don't know how to do the accounting. Do you really think I could make a living doing the bookkeeping for small businesses?"

Mina, YES! I know you can. Once upon a time those big corporations started with just one client. Besides, you could do it on the side until you build your business. You're helping Ellie, right? And you didn't quit your job yet. You, my dear, can do anything you put your heart into."

"Oh, Mom, this feels so exciting, so doable, so right!" Mina felt like a million bricks had been lifted off her shoulders. She could literally feel her heart expanding and glowing.

Sheila could see it, too, and holding in a giggle, asked herself, "How in the hell can someone not see that helping people with their accounting was not healing?"

CHAPTER 11

Mina woke from the deepest sleep she had experienced in months. She almost felt like a new woman as she sat up in bed and stretched her arms out wide. It was still early and the sun was just beginning to peek through the window. The house was so quiet, so still, and so comfortable as if it were giving Mina a great big hug. Mina put on her robe and quietly walked into the kitchen to put a pot of water on the stove for morning tea. She was surprised to see her mother sitting on the deck doing her prayer work. It reminded Mina of the mornings when she was growing up to walk in and see Meme doing her morning prayer work. Mina didn't want to disturb her mom, so she quietly opened the front door to get the paper.

The morning air was crisp and clean as Mina breathed it in deeply and slowly. Her mind was a million miles away as she headed back to the house when suddenly she felt something cold pressed up against her back.

"Walk slowly back into the house without making a scene, or I'll stab you right here and now, you stupid bitch!"

Mina new that voice and fear froze her still.

"Move, I said" Mina tried to not look suspicious as she walked slowly towards her front door. Mina's fear went to a whole new level when she remembered that her mother was on the deck. Mina knew that she would survive this; she'd done it before with him but what would he do to her mom?

"Get your ass inside that house! Did you really think that you could just run away and hide from me forever?"

Mina's deepest fears were coming to life. Brock had found her and he was beyond insane.

"What do you want from me, Brock? We obviously had nothing in common when we dated. You wanted to go out all the time and I wanted to stay home. You liked to drink and I liked to read. That was not a compatible relationship and you know that."

Brock pushed Mina on the couch. "You selfish bitch! All you can think of is yourself. I gave up my life to come save you, to be with you and all you can think of is how you felt? We were good together!"

At that moment, Sheila opened the French doors from the deck. Brock turned in surprise while stepping closer to Mina pointing the knife at her neck.

"One step closer and I'll slit her throat!"

Sheila stopped in her tracks and glared straight at Brock.

"Look who it is! The infamous county psycho witch! What in the hell are you doing here? You know I've never seen you in person only pictures and heard that crazy stories of you. You're really not that scary, you know? Get over here and sit down, NOW!"

Sheila walked steadily and sat down next to Mina.

Mina felt so guilty as the last thing she ever wanted was for Sheila to know about Brock let alone be in a dangerous situation with him. Mina had to protect her mom! Mina stood up to approach Brock but he raised his arm and backhanded her across her face and she fell right back into the couch.

Sheila didn't even flinch. "Brock" She said in a calm voice, "there is not need to be violent. You obviously spent time and effort to find Mina. What exactly do you want?"

"That bitch is coming back with me. She doesn't get to just leave. We are a couple. We belong together, and we will be together forever–even if I have to tie you to the house so you don't run off again!" Brock screamed as he waved the knife at Mina's face.

Mina was scared to death and yet could feel Sheila's calmness and control.

Unbeknownst to Mina, Sheila had been in these situations before, and she knew what to do. Even though neither Brock nor Mina could tell, Sheila was doing her prayer work right in front of them. Sheila had called in her team of Archangels and Elevated Others to help ease the tension of the situation and to guide her actions and words to deescalate Brock. Sheila also imagined Ellie, asking her to come to Mina's house immediately and bring the police.

Brock was getting more and more nervous as he did not count on having two women to deal with. In his plan, he was just going to come and get Mina to take her home. He knew she was sorry for leaving and that she was just too embarrassed to come back. He was helping her see what she really wanted. He knew in his mind that she really loved him and that he was the best thing for her. She was a woman who just needed to be told what to do and where to do it. It was the best thing for her.

"Damnit Mina. Get up and get dressed. We are going back home now!" Brock screamed at her as he motioned with the knife in his hand.

"Brock, do you really think that's the best thing to do at this point, to take Mina back to the same town that she left you? You know as well as I do that people gossip there. Why don't you consider making a life here, away from the past, away from the gossipers?" Sheila said in that ever calming voice.

Mina yelled "What in the hell are you talking about, Mom? I don't ever want to be with this man again!"

"MOM? Crazy psycho witch is your mother?! Holy Shit! I knew you were a little off, but this?" Brock rubbed his forehead wondering what the hell he was going to do now. Going back to Greene County with Mina was going to cause enough of an embarrassment to him, but for people to know he's shacking up with the county witch was a whole other thing!

"Like I said, Brock, have you considered starting a life here with her? You said you wanted to be with her, right? It's a big city; you could easily find a job here. People don't know you here or care if she's related to me. Mina obviously has a nice home that's big enough for you two to share. Where would you live back there? Aren't you still staying with your parents?"

Sheila was apparently calming Brock down as she could see he was really considering the situation. Mina was beginning to see that Sheila was trying to keep him calm while stalling, but stalling for what?

"Brock," Sheila continued, "We are expecting company for tea this morning so if she shows up I don't want you to be startled. Her name is Ellie, she's an old friend of mine I came to the city to meet."

"Well, call her and tell her you are sick or something. Make her not come," Brock yelled.

"I can try her home, but she doesn't have a cell phone and she should be here any minute. Do you want me to try to call her?"

"NO! You'll just call the cops!"

"Brock, I'm not going to call the cops, but Ellie isn't in the best of health, and I don't want to put her in this stressful condition."

Mina was sitting quietly in the chair trying to stay calm as Sheila controlled the seemingly escalating situation. The last thing she wanted was for Ellie to be caught in the middle of her past. She was already feeling so guilty for Sheila being a part of it; though, honestly, she was so very glad she was here. Mina had no idea what she would have done if she were alone with Brock right now.

Mina jumped as the doorbell rang. Oh no, it was Ellie. How was she going to get her to go away without adding to Brock's tension?

"Brock, that's Ellie. I told you she would be here shortly."

"Go answer the door, bitch. Tell her you aren't feeling good or something. Just get her to go away" Brock said.

"Brock, why don't you go tell her that I'm not feeling well and that I'm still in bed? If she sees me, she'll know I'm lying and knowing her she would insist on coming in. Just go to the door and ask her to come back in an hour." Sheila instructed.

Like a kindergarten student, Brock obeyed Sheila and walked towards the door. He could still see Sheila and Mina from his point of view and wanting to scare them from doing something stupid, he lifted up his shirt showing them that he had a gun in his belt. The girls didn't move a muscle. Sheila was still perfectly calm and Mina was shaking, mentally and physically. While Brock slowly opened the door to greet Ellie, he was forming his sentences in his head so they sounded convincing.

This wasn't at all what he had planned for this morning. It was supposed to be a glorious reunion with the love of his life. He would knock on her door and she would jump into his arms, grateful he had rescued her from the horrific life in the city. He brought the knife and gun just in case he needed to protect them as they escaped the horrible surroundings.

With the knife in his hand that was behind the door, Brock opened the door and started to greet Ellie, "Good –"

"Police!"

The door swung open, revealing the knife Brock was concealing. "Drop the knife! Hands in the air! Drop the knife!" the policewoman shouted.

Brock started to step back, looking around while that damn lady kept screaming at him. He was so confused.

"DROP the knife!" she shouted again.

He couldn't think straight. He lunged for her to shut her up! "Shut up, just shut up!" he was screaming in his head. Then a loud bang pierced his thoughts. He kept moving towards her and heard another loud bang. What the hell is that noise? Everything went dark and his dead body fell to the ground.

The police officer leaned down to check Brock's

pulse. When she realized there wasn't one, she walked in to check on Mina and Sheila.

"Mom! Mom, I'm so sorry." Mina cried as she wrapped her arms around her mother.

"Shh, shh. It's okay Mina. It's okay. I'm here." Sheila hugged and tried to comfort her child, her baby girl.

Ellie came busting in "Are you guys Okay?"

"Oh Ellie, thank you! Thank you for hearing my pleas." Sheila said. She looked towards the ceiling and said "Thank you, team, for always being there for me! Thank you for saving us again!"

All three women were in one big hug of gratitude, comforting each other. The policewoman had called for backup and the ambulance. Suddenly there were swarms of people everywhere. One police officer was taking Mina's testimony; one was taking Sheila's while Ellie was fixing hot tea for all.

Ellie smiled to herself thinking "How can someone believe that magic was not involved this morning?"

CHAPTER 12

ina sat on the couch with her arms wrapped around her knees as they pressed against her chest; her life flashing before her eyes. A flood of painful memories was welling up and burning her throat as she sobbed uncontrollably. She felt the wretched pain of the little girl who was left at Meme's house where being with her grandmother went from joy and exuberance to grief and abandonment as her own mother walked away; questioning every single thing school and religion was shoving into her brain; humiliation from being called fat and excluded from friendships in school; being in college, drinking way too much just to fit in. All Mina ever wanted was to belong, to fit in and that had eluded her no matter what she tried. She finally had a boyfriend, yet he beat the hell out of her until she was strong enough to leave. Now, he had just threatened her life and her mother's. The truth hit her in the face, hard: she had wanted to belong, to be loved by choice, not because she was just dropped off to be raised or because she was family and it was expected, but to be wanted so badly that it almost killed her.

Sheila had gathered some candles, her crystals, and her beads to begin prayer work for her daughter, her friend, and honestly, for herself. Sheila had known she was to be with Mina for a visit, but she had no idea what would transpire. Most of the time, when Sheila was intuitively led to a place or person, she had some idea of the reason, whether it's an illness, money, a loved one passing or assisting in their spiritual up-leveling. Sheila actually thought the reason she was feeling the urge to be with Mina was that it was time for Mina to take over the family business. Now all she wanted to do was hold her baby and comfort her through this horrific time. However, she felt that right now the last thing Mina wanted was the lady who abandoned her long ago to suddenly wrap her arms around her and promise everything would be okay.

Mina felt like she had sobbed for hours and, yet, there was still so much anger left inside. She looked up to realize that Ellie had left and that her mother had lit some candles, placed crystals in a grid and was chanting over her beads.

"Dammit, MOM!" Mina screamed "is that all you do? Light candles, put some stupid rocks around, and chant prayers? I'm almost died today, and I'm dying inside! What? Do you not have some place to run off to? Do you need me to call you a cab? Is your broomstick broken that you can't just fly away at the very point I need you the most? I hate . . . everything! I hate magic, I hate you, I hate myself!"

Sheila immediately went to Mina's side and put her arms around her, holding her tight, sobbing herself. "I know, Mina. Saying I'm sorry won't help but I am so very sorry. I thought I was doing the right thing. I had convinced myself that I would be the last of the Greene County witches that times had changed so much that no one would ever need to call on you. I had in my mind that I was doing this for you, breaking the family tradition so that you could have a normal life. I was trying to protect you." They sat sobbing for several minutes, then, in silence for hours held each other - Sheila loving on her daughter, trying to make up for all the years she should have been there, Mina being loved by her mother trying, to erase the loneliness of her life.

CHAPTER 13

Early Monday morning, Mina crawled out of bed feeling like her body was 100 years old. There was no way she would be able to function at the office and since she had several days of vacation, she called and left a message on her supervisor's phone that she would be out all week. Mina was really surprised at the level of relief she felt not having to go to work. Even though her job duties were mindless, Mina liked everyone there. In truth she didn't have that strong of a bond with any of them. She doubted anyone would even miss her and she knew she wouldn't miss them.

Mina felt like she had lived a lifetime in the last two days, a hard lifetime. Her mind hurt, her body hurt and her heart was in a million pieces. She could barely comprehend what had happened since Sheila showed up. Mina had started to soften the strains of her mother/daughter relationship and was beginning to see her mother as a person not a She-Devil; she had learned that her mother knew and worked with Ellie; her abusive ex-boyfriend not only found where she lived but showed up trying to kidnap her and ended up dead! It felt more like three lifetimes in two days. Mina was amazed that she even thought of calling into the office.

Still very raw, Mina slowly walked into the kitchen to make tea. She was not surprised to see Sheila doing her morning prayer work on the deck. Mina instantly had more feelings rush to her mind and cut into her heart. She was still so pissed at this woman yet so very grateful she was with her through the actual toughest part of her life and so fearful that Sheila would be leaving any moment. Mina tried to swallow another sob. She had cried so much in the last twelve hours she was afraid if she let one small sob out she would not be able to stop the avalanche of others that would surely follow.

As Mina mindlessly poured a cup of hot tea from her Meme's teapot, Sheila came in from the deck. Sheila could see from the look in Mina's eyes that she had cried most of the night. Sheila didn't know whether to hug her daughter or keep her distance.

"Good morning, Mina" was all she could say as she was standing frozen waiting for Mina's wrath to start again. Sheila knew in her heart that she deserved every single hateful and hurtful thing that Mina would say. Sheila had said them a million times to herself.

"Good morning, Mom. Would you like a cup of tea?" Mina replied in a soft but guarded tone.

"Oh, yes, please. That sounds wonderful right now".

Sheila clasped her hot cup of tea and followed Mina to the living room to sit down in the chair across from her.

"Mom, what exactly do you do? Do you fly all over the world saving people like you did me yesterday?" Mina asked.

"Well, Mina, I must say, yesterday wasn't like any typical day I've ever had. Each day, each person, each situation is different. One client may request that I pray with them as their loved one passes. I may spend a week with another client teaching them how to communicate with their pets. In other cases, I have spent months helping a person work through their illness on a different level than just medicine. I've spent an hour delivering a message to someone from their ancestors. In a nutshell, I show people how to bring magic into their daily lives."

"I must say, Mom, I hate that word, 'magic'. It reminds me of some person on a stage doing fake illusions."

"Oh, I know, Mina. It doesn't seem to mean the same thing today as it did generations ago. To me, magic means being outside the box of normal. Why not ask our loved ones who have crossed over for guidance? We are all energy and just because they have left this dimension doesn't mean we can't still converse with them. Every time you think of someone or something, here or who have crossed over, you are communicating in some way."

"Meme taught me that everything is energy and everything has a soul, so I get that. I mean, she was always talking to her plants and animals. I guess I just didn't realize they were talking back."

"Did you ever see Meme give a plant a teaspoon of vinegar, Mina?" asked Sheila.

"Actually, yes. She would say that the plant asked for it. I just thought she looked at the leaves and thought they had bugs or something. But you're saying that the plant really did ask for vinegar, Mom?"

"What I'm saying is that Meme listened to the plant as it was telling her she was off balance and Meme knew what to give the plant to make her flourish. If Meme hadn't listened to the plant, she wouldn't have known what to do. It could have just been that Meme walked by the plant and had a thought that the plant needed vinegar and Meme gave it to her. No big deal. That is actually communicating with the plant. People make it out to be something so very weird when they think of talking to plants, trees, pets, jewelry, anything. It really is no big deal, all you have to do is follow through with the thoughts and ideas you receive. That's how God, Angels, the Elevated Others, and ancestors communicate, too." Sheila explained.

Mina sat there feeling deep down in her soul that this was the truth, her truth.

Mina said, "Honestly, I have started talking with my angels and acknowledging their assistance. It really does feel good. Better than good. I feel the love that I have so longed for when I connect with them. That love and acceptance is what I thought I was missing out from you leaving me with Meme. But it's deeper than that. It's a love that even when I'm with Meme, I'm still longing for. As soon as I connect with Spirit and ground into Mother Earth, I feel like I'm on a high that nothing else could quench. All these years I thought it was you I was missing, and it was, but what I'm understanding now is that I was really missing my connection to the Universe!" "And that Mina is what magic is all about. It's everything outside of normal."

CHAPTER 14

Mina couldn't believe how exhausted she had felt the last couple of days. She felt like her limbs weighed a 100 pounds each. She had experienced a whole spectrum of feelings, from crying to giggling, to sobbing to laughing and hours of just staring into space. Mina didn't know what to do next. She felt like she just didn't fit anywhere anymore. In her heart, Mina knew that as bad as last weekend was, somehow it would be the catalyst to change her soul had longed for.

"Mom, I just don't know what to do next," Mina said as the two of them sat on the deck enjoying the nice weather. "Going back to the office is just so heavy. I mean, when I think of it I can hardly breathe. It's so weird because everyone was nice to work with and the job wasn't hard. Hell, I could do it in my sleep. I just can't see me walking in there every day accomplishing absolutely nothing. I just don't feel like I belong anywhere."

"Well, dear, sometimes the hardest thing is to

navigate a new normal. Let's try again with the things you know you don't want to do," Sheila replied.

"I can do better than that, Mom. I know what I want to do. I don't have it all figured out but I know what makes my heart sing. I love everything about the store. Ellie's store." Mina's eyes and face lit up as she began to talk about helping Ellie with her financials and getting the inventory in line. "Mom, I love numbers. Like I said before, how structured they are, so definite, you know, and two plus two always equals four. And I love working with people, not just stuck in some back office running a calculator. I get excited at the thought of helping people not be afraid of their money. Small businesses can't always afford to hire a big time accountant to help them, so they just push it to the side month after month, leaving the piles of invoices and bank statements until the paperwork is so overwhelming they don't have the time to tackle it. I believe that's one of the reasons so many small businesses fail, they don't have the time or knowledge to produce a solid financial statement. If you don't know where you are, how will you know where to go?"

Sheila was grinning from ear to ear watching Mina light up with excitement. Sheila knew that Mina was truly connecting with what her soul was saying.

Mina plopped down on the lounge chair next to her mother, all of the excitement immediately drained from her being. "Mom, I can't do that. I have no idea how to make a living on helping small businesses. How would I even go about getting more clients to hire me? How would I even find the time to meet other business owners. I just don't know how to do any of it. I guess it's a good thing I still have a job to go to." Sheila put her arms around her daughter to comfort her. "Mina, the one thing I am more certain of than anything is that the 'how' is not up to us."

"What? I have to know how to go about getting clients and how to make this happen. You can't just have a dream and no steps to accomplishing it," Mina said firmly.

"I can promise you, Mina, that if you tell the Universe that this is what you want, the way you want to be of service, the clients will come. All that Spirit asks of us is to know what you want and leave the how up to the Universe! Think about it this way, if you limit the way God can answer your prayers by saying exactly how you want things to show up, it would take the angels years to synchronize that. And if you just focus on the end result, the feelings you want to experience with this prayer, it will happen in ways you could not dream of. When you worry about the 'how' you are limiting the ways your blessings show up. For example, see yourself getting ready in the morning to go meet a new client, feel the excitement of a new challenge, hear the teapot on the stove ready for your morning tea before your walk out the door, see the new suit you put on that goes so amazingly with your new shoes, feel the gratitude for the money to buy the outfit and the perfect necklace to just makes the entire ensemble sparkle, see your gas tank full as you start your car to begin your next adventure. Then, smile as you give thanks for the amazingly unique way this client came to you, a way you could never have dreamed of. This is 'how' you co-create what you really want, big or small."

"So, like when I'm talking with my angels and ask them for a parking spot? You know, I do actually 'see' the parking spot in front of a store when I ask them. I never realized that I don't say, 'Hey, can you make that red car parked in front of the store check out and move their car so I can have that spot'? I just see the spot open and ninety-nine percent of the time the spot is available exactly where I see it. Hmmm. I never thought of it like that. And, you're right, getting tangled up in the 'how' is so exhausting."

Mina stared out over the deck contemplating all that she had just realized.

"By allowing God to take care of the how is actually trusting that the Universe has your back," Sheila replied. "Like, trusting that me following my soul's calling meant that you would be safe, loved, and would one day understand that by my doing so would help you find your calling. I knew in my heart that if I stayed and raised you, it would be detrimental to both of our souls," Sheila said as a tear rolled down her cheek.

"Last week, Mom, I would have never believed that. Now I know it's true with a capital T! I love you, Mom."

"I love you too, Mina."

CHAPTER 15

Mina felt so high after the conversation with her mom that she could not contain the urge to drive to Ellie's store. She needed to get out of the house, get in her car and drive. She wanted to start back on Ellie's financials again. Yes, she felt like she needed to thank Ellie for saving her and her mom's life but the feeling of actually taking a step towards her dream was catapulting her past the fear and shame of Ellie knowing about Brock. Sheila had told Mina several times that he wasn't her fault and that it took more strength than she knew to survive him, twice. Shame was part of her shadow work for Mina and would be for some time but she knew in her heart that she had made massive steps forward with the help of her mother.

Mina got dressed and as she was walking out the door, told Sheila she would be back in a few hours. They both knew that time flew when you were doing what you loved so no false promises were given. Mina walked out her front door, closed it behind her, and stopped, standing right where the policewoman had stood when she took Brock's life. If that woman was scared, she didn't show it that day. Mina took in a long, deep breath and stepped forward dramatically knowing that the step was heading her to her new life, new goals, new future.

Mina sat in the car and did her usual parking lot communication with the Angels, asking and thanking them for their help. Mina pulled out of the drive and headed to Ellie's store and continued her conversation with her Angels.

"I really want to be of service, I mean, not like Mom does or anything, but I want to help people. And I'm really good at numbers! I want to help business owners around the country succeed at what they do. I can't imagine how many people Ellie's store has helped and if she were to close, think how many others wouldn't get to experience it. If I can help people keep following their dreams of owning a successful and profitable business, which would be my dream, my dream of helping others with their dream! I know the 'how' is up to you, but can you help point me in the right direction, put the right people in my path, and give me the courage to take the step and offer my abilities? I'm grateful that I have put money away for a rainy day. That rainy day was the fear that Brock would turn up again and I'd have to run and hide. I don't want that money to be for fear. I want that money to help me help others. I have a spare bedroom - well, when Mom's not using it - but I can turn that into an office for now. I can go meet the clients at their establishments, so no worry about someone I don't really know coming to my house. I can get a post office box for my business address." Mina's mind was going a hundred miles an hour as she pulled up to the empty parking spot in front of Ellie's store. "Thank you for the amazing parking spot, again. Funny, I don't feel one bit guilty for always getting the best spot in the lot!"

Mina walked into the store with a whole new perspective, not only because she and Ellie had shared something so traumatic or because the items in the store had a totally different meaning but because Mina knew in her heart that she was doing exactly what she was called to do – be of service. Ellie hurried to the door and gave Mina the biggest hug, a hug of sympathy and gratitude and a knowing of a deeper connection the two could never have foreseen.

"Mina, it is so very good to see you. You look radiant! How have you been? It seems like years since we've seen you." Ellie was obviously giving a hint that Savannah knew nothing of their connection over the past few days.

Savannah was hot on Ellie's heels rushing over to hug Mina too. Savannah felt like Mina was a sister from another lifetime.

"Hi Mina! So glad you came in today. I have missed you, too" Savannah said as she gave Mina a big hug.

Mina laughed to herself, realizing that the total energy between the three had changed, had gone to another level and she was grateful. Mina knew that once Sheila left, Ellie and Savannah would be her family in the city. Man, did that pull on her heart – the thought of mom leaving again. It made Mina's heart skip a beat but she pushed it down to deal with later.

"Let's get back to those financials, shall we, Ellie?"

llie moaned and Savannah squealed, "Yay! There's some new products I'd like to bring in but Ellie says we need to talk to you first. Something about under-standing the inventory" Savannah was laughing as they all walked towards the back room.

"The only thing that has changed is that the stacks are a bit bigger" Ellie joked. "I tried to keep them organized into the piles you left. Hopefully that will help a bit."

Mina took off her jacket and got started working on creating a spreadsheet for the store's inventory.

She knew that Ellie needed a clear picture of what was selling vs. what wasn't, categories, price points, quality versus quantity, all things in Mina's wheelhouse. She put her head down and got to work, and the other two obviously left the area but Mina didn't notice.

After what seemed like ten minutes to Mina, three hours had passed. Mina stood up and stretched her shoulders and neck as she walked to find Ellie.

"Hey, Ellie," Mina called. "Can you come and take a look at some of the stuff I have found?"

Ellie's heart sank as she instantly felt like she was being called to the principal's office. Ellie felt like such a failure when it came to managing the financials of her business. When she got into this, she convinced herself that it would be just like running her household bills would come in and she would pay them, simple as that. Man, oh man, was she kidding herself. She just knew that Mina was going to tell her either to sell the store or go get another loan to stay afloat, neither of which would be easy.

Mina could feel the fear in Ellie as she put her arm around her. "Ellie, it's not that bad, really. I think you are going to be surprised at what I have found."

The two ladies walked to the back room where Mina had all the information she needed to present to Ellie a couple of viable options. Savannah was trying to be sly and stand as close to the door as possible to hear the outcome. Savannah loved this store as much as Ellie.

Mina whispered to Ellie "Do you care if we include her, too?"

"I guess it's okay. I might as well be shamed in front of her, too." Ellie replied.

"Shamed? I would never do that! And I think you value Savannah's input or you wouldn't have let her run your shop, right?" Ellie nodded in agreement as Mina said to Savannah "Aren't you coming too?"

Savannah's face beamed and she hurried to their sides.

Mina handed the ladies a printout of numbers that looked like garble to Ellie but Savannah was going over them with a fine-tooth comb.

Mina started her presentation: "Ladies, you have done an amazing job of making this store profitable. And I believe it can be more profitable with a few tweaks. It appears that your inventory levels are well supported by the sales. There are a couple of categories I would suggest you try to find different vendors who offer the same or better quality for a cheaper price, or, go back to your current vendors and try to negotiate a better deal. I can do that for you and teach you how to do that while maintaining a great relationship with the companies. Also, it seems that your electric is a bit high. There are a couple of suggestions I have for that if you are interested."

Both girls were eagerly shaking their heads yes urging Mina to continue with her brilliance.

"First, are there lights you leave on at night when the store is closed?"

"Yes. The front windows stay lit all night and a light over the back reading nook to deter robbers." Ellie replied.

"Ok, and those in the front are neon and the whole strip has lights that are under the awnings pointed to the front of the store, correct?"

"Yes."

Mina continued "How about if you turn off the window lights and allow for the awning lights to shine?" Ellie and Savannah looked intrigued. How did they not think of this? Would it look like the store was a dark hole? Mina could see them questioning the suggestion. "All I'm asking is that you try it. If you don't like the way it feels with the neon window lights off, try turning off half of them. If you dobn't like that either, leave them all on. These are just suggestions. I do agree that one light in the reading nook should stay on. Let's make sure that's an LED bulb. In fact, let's make sure all of the lights are LED bulbs. It may seem like a bit out of pocket up front but you will see a difference in the electric bill. I have also noticed that the classrooms are lit when they aren't being used. How would you feel about turning those off unless there are classes in there?"

Both ladies nodded their heads in agreement.

After about an hour of Mina giving different ideas on how to save money, she directed their attention to the profit and loss statement she handed them. Both ladies looked confused as Mina started to explain the information.

"Guys, what this piece of paper shows is that you are doing an amazing job with this business. That number at the bottom is the profit you are making this year!"

"Profit?" Ellie asked.

"Yes, profit. And with what we have been going over, I feel that there is room to make an even bigger profit by the end of the year!"

Ellie and Savannah jumped out of the seats, hands in the air cheering. Mina could actually see the weight of the world leaving Ellie's face. Savannah was in the "I told you so" mode. They all three laughed and celebrated the great news. Mina could feel her soul singing. She looked up and thanked God, the Universe and her angels for being able to realize her gift. And in that moment she knew with all of her heart, this is what she was called to do.

As the three were laughing and talking about expanding the goods and services of the store, Mina's phone rang. She picked it up to see "SheDevil" on the caller ID. Mina laughed to herself.

"Damn, I need to change that, don't I?"

"Hey Mom" Mina answered. "What's up?"

There was something in her mother's tone that made Mina's heart sink into her stomach.

"What's wrong, Mom? Yeah, I'm pretty much done here. I'll head home right away." Mina hung up and tried to smile to the girls. "Well, I think we are done here for now. Let's meet up next week to discuss some avenues to branch out. Deal?"

"Deal!" Ellie and Savannah replied in unison.

Mina gathered her things and tried to pretend that everything was still jubilant. She gave the girls a hug and headed home. This was it, Mina thought. This was when mom had to leave to go to her next client. Mina had known in her heart that this day would come. Why did her heart ache so badly? She and her mother had healed a lifetime of grief in the last couple of days. Mina wasn't ready for Sheila to leave. Mina loved seeing her mom on her deck each morning doing the prayer work that she had seen Meme do so long ago.

"I know, I know. I can call her any time," Mina said out loud as a tear ran down her cheek.

It wouldn't be like before where Mina avoided any contact with Sheila. That ache in her heart was the same horrible feeling Mina felt as the little girl waiting on the step for her mom to come home, promising to be a good girl if she would just come back. Mina pulled into her driveway, put the car in park and just cried her eyes out. She couldn't go in yet. She wasn't ready for her mom to leave again. Who would have thought that just a few days ago Mina was dreading even having lunch with her. This cry was so deep, so heart wrenching, Mina realized it was her inner little girl releasing all that pent up anger, resentment and loneliness. Dammit, hadn't she cried enough? Mina wiped her tears, adjusted her make up and opened the car door. "Let's get this over with. I can cry later." she said to herself as she walked in the front door.

"Mom, what's going on? Your voice sounded kinda down. I guess you are onto your next client, huh?" Mina asked.

"Oh, Honey, it's not my next client. It's Meme," Sheila responded releasing a sob that she had been trying so hard to hold in. "I have to leave immediately to be with her. Can you please take me to the car rental place? I called for them to bring me one but it will take two hours. I need to go now."

"Yes, Mom. I'll take you. Why don't you let me just drive you home myself? I'm done with my obligations here for now. Please let me take you."

Sheila shook her head in agreement as tears ran down her face, actually both of their faces had tear stains. Not another word was exchanged as Mina put together a suitcase of essentials while Sheila packed the car. When everything was ready, Mina locked the door and got in the driver's seat next to her mother. As Mina took her mother's hand she could feel the love, longing and grief her mother was feeling about her own mother. "Distance does not break the bond of love", Mina thought to herself as they drove towards the highway to Meme.

CHAPTER 16

With one hand on the wheel and one hand holding her mother's, Mina drove as fast as she could towards Meme's house. Man, it had been way too long since she'd been there. Meme was so much a part of Mina's life even though they were miles apart. Mina's favorite color was lavender, and she knew that was because Meme's bedroom was that most beautiful shade of purple. Lavender made Mina feel safe and loved, no matter if it was the color, the smell, or just the name. Meme was the matriarch of this family. She was tough and stubborn as well as loving and nurturing to people, plants, animals and birds. Meme had been Mina's rock when her mother left. She tried to so hard to fill the hole in Mina's life when her mom left. Only recently did Mina realize that Meme had intimately known Mina's heartbreak as well as Sheila's broken heart.

Sheila was lost in thought along the drive. Her mind was racing so much that she didn't even realize that the two of them hadn't spoken a word in over a hundred miles. What would she do without her mother, again? She and Gladys had had their differences for sure, not unlike she and Mina had. Sheila had resented her mother for years and years. Yet, when it came time to make for her to take on the family business, the first person she turned to was her mom to raise Mina. Of course, Sheila made Gladys promise to raise Mina as normal as possible and her mom fulfilled that promise and more. Sheila didn't realize how much their relationship had healed and strengthened each day when she would call about Mina. Even after Mina had grown, left for college and moved to the city, Sheila continued to call her mom daily for advice, strength, appreciation, support and love. Little did Sheila realize, Gladys felt the same way.

"Mom, you okay?" Mina asked as she squeezed Sheila's hand.

Sheila's mind was far away but snapped back when Mina spoke. "Yes, Honey. I was just lost in thought reminiscing. How about you?". "I'm okay. I was doing the same thing. I was sure you were praying to God or talking to some spirit or something."

"Oh, I've been doing prayer work, don't think I haven't. I was just thinking how far Mom and I have come over the years. She is my best friend in the world, my confidant, my cheerleader, my big shoulder to cry on. I knew yesterday when we spoke that something was up."

"I didn't know you spoke to her yesterday, Mom" Mina replied.

"Yep, we speak every single day. Sometimes it is for five minutes sometimes for hours but we talk each day. She made me stronger, more passionate about healing. I know this sounds weird but when we connected she amped up my connection to Spirit. It's like her words blew the clouds of confusion and doubt away so that I could clearly see what God was trying to show me. We would talk about the messages we were getting and how we were getting them.

"We talked about you, our family, our traditions. We could spend hours talking about how structured religions really weren't all that different yet were so far from what we knew as truth."

Mina glanced at her with that questioning look, asking "and what was your conclusion?"

Sheila chuckled "Oh, we had many thoughts on the subject, but mainly that God is a loving God, not fear-based. That the main theme in all religions is love: love for yourself, love for others and that love doesn't know distances. People get so caught up in who's doing what right or wrong, judging everything and everyone. Meme and I agreed in our feelings that we are all made of energy and everything is living, everything has a spirit and with that, God is in EVERY SINGLE thing. If we could all just see that, everything would be different."

"Yeah, I get that. But it's hard to understand that God was there with Brock when he beat me to a pulp and when he was trying to kidnap me."

"I can understand from a point of view that Brock was pure evil. I can also look behind the curtain of the physical and acknowledge that God had a hand in us surviving. Brock made choices and each choice has consequences.

"You can't tell me that the angels didn't relay the message to Ellie or that the Universe didn't orchestrated me being there with you. If I hadn't listened to the messages I was receiving from Spirit to come see you, I shudder at the thought of what might have happened. I'm not saying I saved the day, I'm just saying as a mom, I'm so glad I was there with you."

"I'm glad you were there with me too, Mom. I'm sorry I wasn't very nice to you. I really am sorry." Mina shook her head feeling ashamed at how she had treated her mom for years.

"Honey, it's okay. I promise. I understood more than you could have realized.

I'm so grateful to Meme for raising you to be the

amazing woman you have become. She is so proud of you."

Feeling more ashamed Mina replied "I should have called her more, come back here more often. I'm not a very good granddaughter."

"Oh yes you are, my dear. Your Meme knew that she had raised you to be independent. How could she feel anything but pride when you left to tackle this world on your own? Meme often said she could not do the things you do, live in a big city where you know no one. She said she couldn't have done the things I did, flying all over the world in sometimes dangerous situations to help someone. I would remind her that I could not do what she had done. One day, I'll share some of the amazing stories of Meme's life. Talk about God given abilities to heal! She is my inspiration for sure."

As the car got closer to Meme's home, the conversations quieted as both had drifted back to the thoughts going on in their own heads. What would they do without Meme? Who would take care of the homestead? That place had been in the family for many generations and most of them still buried in the family cemetery on the hill. Mina and Sheila simultaneously took a deep breath as they turned into the driveway, feeling anxious to hug Meme yet wishing they could delay the inevitable reality.

Mina could barely get the car in park before her mom opened the door and ran towards the house. Sheila threw open the screen door of the back porch and ran inside.

"Mom! Mom!" was all Mina could hear as she got out of the car and followed her own mother inside.

In an instant, all three women were together in Meme's lavender room. Gladys was lying in bed with handmade quilts keeping her warm. As Mina and Sheila took Meme's hands, the three joined together, and a deep love was shared between them. It was almost tangible, not just the feeling of the hands but the feeling of the energy running to and through each one.

Gladys opened her eyes and smiled "My girls! Oh, how I love my girls." She gently squeezed each of their hands and closed her eyes again.

"Mom, we are here with you. Do you need anything?" Sheila asked.

As Mina looked at her mother, she could see a five-year-old girl crying for her mom not to go away. Mina knew that look and felt that hurt to her core. Mina felt like she was five years old going through that same abandonment again. This time, instead of hating her mom, holding in her own sobs, Mina's whole being hurt for Sheila.

"No, Honey" Gladys replied, "just knowing you two are here is all I could have wished for."

"We are here with you Meme. We aren't going anywhere" Mina replied.

"Mom, its okay for you to go if you feel you are ready. You know we love you and we know you love us."

Gladys whispered "Every time you think of me, I'm right there with you. Love doesn't know distance." Sheila had tears streaming down her face "When I see a red cardinal, I'll know it's you. Please visit often."

Mina, trying her hardest to hold in the sobs said "Meme, thank you for all you have done for me. I wouldn't be the woman I am now without you. Every time I see lavender, I'm reminded of how loved and safe I am."

"I love you dear Mina. I'm so very proud of you. For me, please follow your heart, find your passion and live your days your way. I'm always with you both."

Meme drifted back to sleep. As the three sat in silence, Meme's breath began to labor.

They were still holding Meme's hands as each breath was feared to be the last. All of the sudden, the room got brighter and filled with an indescribable calm. Mina and Sheila looked at each other and then around the room. Even though they were still holding Meme's hands, they could see her spirit sit up and walk to the side of the room. She was dressed in a flowing gown filled with white sequins; her head had a crown that sparkled brighter than the sun. Gladys reached out to take the Archangel Michael's hand as she looked back and winked at the girls. In the next instant Gladys and the angel disappeared as the room dimmed from the absence of the light. Mina and Sheila looked back at each other confirming they both saw what just happened. As they looked at Meme's body, they knew she had already taken her last breath. Meme had crossed the bridge to Heaven.

CHAPTER 17

Mina and Sheila sat holding each other as each one began grieving and celebrating Meme, both lost in their own thoughts yet tears streaming down each face. Mina wanted to be strong for her mom yet she just couldn't let go of the secure embrace of her mother. Sheila knew there were tons of things to be done and yet she couldn't let go of the loving hug of security from her daughter. If they were to ever look back they would realize that this was the very moment their entire relationship changed.

What seemed like hours later Meme's house was all abuzz with women every where. The funeral home had come for the body in preparation for the ceremony on the hill side. Meme would be buried with the rest of her family. Even though the casket would be closed the perfect outfit had been picked along with Meme's treasured accessories. Mina was so surprised that the macaroni bracelet she had made Meme years ago was among those prized accessories.

"Mom, what all is going with Meme?"

"There was a list of things that Meme wanted with her, treasures that were close to her heart and she felt only meant something to her. The beloved bracelet you had made her, her wedding band that she never took off and a crystal necklace I had given her a few years back. She was adamant that her eagle feather go with her as well as her turtle shell."

Mina gave Sheila a strange look when Sheila told her about the eagle feather and turtle shell.

"Meme was so very grateful for the gifts from the eagle and turtle. She would tell the story of how the eagle plucked its longest tail feather just for Meme as a thank you gift when she nursed it back to health. Meme would say that the message from the eagle was that every time she held the feather, the two of them would be safely flying to a higher place allowing for a different point of view. The turtle was a symbol for Meme that no matter where she was she would be and feel protected and safe, like her home on her back." Sheila smiled. "Meme had thousands of stories like that. That woman was truly gifted at seeing things from a different perspective than most. And she truly enjoyed this life."

Once again both women were distracted by the seeming chaos all around. Where did all those women come from? Who even called them to tell them Meme had passed? Mina didn't think she remembered any of them but they sure buzzed around like they lived there, they knew where everything was. One was baking, one was cleaning, one was in the corner doing prayer work. It was unsettling on one hand yet very comforting on another, knowing that all these years Mina thought Meme was a lonely old lady, Gladys had a ton of very close friends. Mina looked around for Sheila to ask her about all the women but she was nowhere around. That was okay because Mina really needed some fresh air and the garden was calling her.

As Mina walked away from the noisy house to the quiet garden, she could see Meme's handiwork. Every single plant looked like it was the most prized specimen ever. The flowers were all blooming, the vegetables all had blooms or produce growing and the branches of the fruit trees were beginning to bend under the weight of their gifts. It was magical indeed and as Mina strolled through the garden lost in thoughts she noticed two people standing by the barn. Mina walked towards them wondering who they could possibly be and how freaking rude to be sneaking around here today!

As she got closer to the barn, Mina could see that it was her mom talking to some guy. Several things about this were odd to Mina: first, it was the only guy she had seen on this property – every; second, they seemed to be very familiar with each other; third, they clearly were discussing something that was to be private; and the list could go on. Mina couldn't stop. She had to know what was going on and if her mother was in danger.

"Mom," Mina called. Sheila jumped from the sound of Mina's voice. "Mom, are you okay?"

"Oh, yes Mina" she replied realizing that Mina was not going away and she did not want Mina hearing their conversation. "Mina, this is Jonathan. He's an old friend that recently moved back to the area. Jonathan, this is my daughter, Mina."

"Hello, Mina. It's truly a pleasure to meet you. Sheila, it's been great catching up a bit. I hope we can continue our conversation soon. And, Mina, I hope we have the opportunity to connect again before you leave." Jonathan shook both of their hands and walked back through the pasture to what Mina assumed was his property.

"How do you know Jonathan, Mom?"

"He's an old friend that grew up down the road. We spent hours together before life got in the way. He went his way and I followed my passion. I knew he had moved back but I didn't realize he had been helping Meme as much as he had." Sheila explained.

"It's so nice to know that she had so many friends, especially taking care of this place on her own" Mina replied. "What are we going to do with this place, Mom?"

"Well, Mina, Mom left the entire estate to me and you as well as enough money in her safe to sustain this farm for many generations. I know we will need to get into the details more later, but I'm hoping to move here permanently if that's okay with you. I'd like to update the home and possibly start a business using the plants and herbs in creams, soaps and tinctures. You know, have a real home base and still be able to do my magic helping people around the world?" Sheila's eyes lit up with the possibilities but stopped in her tracks "If that's ok with you Mina. I want you to be part of this but I don't want you to be bogged down with it. I want you to fly in the direction of your passion, not just mine." Mina felt instant comfort knowing that the farm would still stay in the family, that she would know exactly where Sheila was and that she was thriving continuing to follow her passion. "Yes, Mom, I think that's a perfect plan. And I must admit, I feel much more comfortable about you being her by yourself knowing that you have help across the pasture should you need it. Jonathan seems like a nice man and you guys seem to have a long-time connection."

"Oh, you have no idea," Sheila thought to herself.

After a few days, the time came for the ceremony. The two walked hand in hand behind the buggy as the horse pulled the casket to the hillside. Mina was in complete amazement to see that there must have been fifty people following them, including Ellie. Meme was well loved by her community, no matter what Brock had called her family. They may have been the Greene County witches but with a flock like that, who would dare mess with them, Mina smiled to herself.

The ceremony was perfectly Meme. The birds were singing, the sun was shining and a soft breeze was blowing as they all gathered to celebrate the woman. The stories of Meme shared by many made Mina completely filled with awe, admiration, strength and love. There was a whole other side to the matriarch of this family that included faith, family, friends and magic. As they all walked back towards the house, Mina saw a big red cardinal sitting on the fence post.

She felt her mom walk up beside her, gently grab her hand and whisper "Love knows no distance," acknowledging the cardinal and the magic shared by the three of them.

The next few days were filled with visits, stories, laughter, cries, and more food than Mina had ever seen. It was truly a celebration of life. Sheila seemed to be finding a new rhythm with the farm and felt truly at home. Mina loved this place more than she ever could imagine. This was her base but it wasn't time for it to be her home. The city was calling her back, not her job, as she had already quit the firm. Her home was calling her. Sheila and Mina both knew it was time for her to head back to the city. One quiet evening the two were sitting outside in Meme's swing.

"Mom, it's time for me to head back to the city," Mina said.

"I know, dear. I've been waiting on you to tell me. Actually, you stayed a few days longer than I expected but loved that you did," Sheila chuckled.

"It's different, Mom. It's all different. You know I don't have a job to go back to but I feel this pull. I have so many things going through my head of what I could do, what I really want to do. I'm so much clearer on that now. I never thought I could support myself doing what I love, helping people in my own way. But if you and Meme taught me anything, it's that being of service is in our blood, no matter what that looks like. I truly feel like I can do anything. I know there will be bumps in the road, but.."

Sheila interrupted "But, I'll be right here to help you see a different perspective and possible solutions. That's what Meme always did for me. She loved me for who I was, for everything I was. No judgment, just love."

"And that's what made us the women we are today." Mina chimed in.

They continued swinging in silence. Mina was ready and Sheila knew it. It was time for her to fly, to return to the city she loved. Thanks to Meme and Sheila, Mina would not return the same woman but stronger, freer and more passionate than ever before.

CHAPTER 18

"**M**omma! Please, please stop the cries from Mina! If I'm going to leave her with you, she has to be soothed! I can't leave like this!" Sheila begs as the cries get louder and louder in her head. "Momma, please stop the baby from crying!"

Sheila is suddenly awakened from her nightmare, drenched in sweat with tears running down her face. Why in the world did this recurring dream shake her to the core every single night? Sheila slowly rose out of her bed to start the teapot on that old familiar stove in the kitchen she and Mina grew up in. Maybe it was because she was spending so much time in this home after her mother had passed just a few weeks ago. There were so many memories in this land and home; this was, in fact, the only home Sheila ever had.

Sheila got dressed and walked back into the kitchen to fix her cup of tea. This combination of tea was her mother's favorite. Gladys always did know just the right mix of herbs and tea leaves to soothe a soul. Sheila could feel the grip around her heart every time she thought of her mother. She longed for just one more long conversation with her mother in the swing under the trees; just one more time for Gladys to chuckle as she shared a story of her prayer work and the unexpected outcomes. Sheila knew that Gladys really had no idea how extremely powerful her magic was. Yes, Gladys had always had that special knack of knowing which plant combination would ease a bee sting or what fruit tree leaf would settle a headache. In Gladys's world, every plant was a gift, a healing tool that deserved to be loved and treasured, even if the plant seemingly just supplied shade over the barn.

Sheila jumped as her cell phone rang and she knew it was Mina without even looking.

"Mom, are you okay?"

"Yes, Mina. I'm fine. What in the world are you doing up at this hour?"

"Mom, my spidey senses told me to call you. Did you have another nightmare?"

"I wouldn't call it a nightmare Mina. I just know that Dream Source is trying to get a message to me and for the life of me I can't figure it out. I can't get past the immense feeling of guilt and sorrow to receive the real message."

"That's it, Mom, I'm heading to the farm. I miss you and Meme terribly and it will do my soul good to be grounded in the land."

"Oh honey, you know I'd love to see you. It just a very long trip for a bad dream and I know you are so very busy with your new clients."

"And that's just the reason I need to slow down and take some time for me. I'll see you in a few hours. Oh, how about I bring some stuff for lunch from your favorite market? Sound good? See you in a few!" Mina didn't even give Sheila a chance to answer before she hung up the phone. One thing was for sure, that girl was stubborn just like her grandmother.

Sheila sat at the kitchen table, slowly sipping on her tea as her she started her prayer work. Each morning, Sheila made a point of starting her day in gratitude. She silently gave thanks to God and Goddess for all things in her life; she gave thanks to the home for it's security; she gave thanks to the fire for it's warmth and light; thanks to the trees, to the land, to the sun and moon; thanks to her Elevated Others and Elevated Ancestors for their guidance and help; thanks to all the other magical beings that had and will cross her path – seen and unseen, known and unknown, magical and mundane - that helped her make this the best day ever;

she thanked the water, the wind and the clouds for all that they provided.

A sudden knock at the door jolted Sheila out of her prayer work. As she headed to the door, she could feel it was friendly and in that moment, she knew it was Jonathan. It had been so good to have his help and company the last few weeks.

"Good morning" Sheila said as she opened the door.

"Is everything okay?" Jonathan asked with a worried look on his face.

"Yes, Jonathan. Everything is fine, here. Are you okay?" Sheila asked.

"Yes. I was just worried when I saw your light on and thought I better come and check on you."

"Since when have I been your responsibility to run and save mister?" Sheila teased him. She really was grateful to see him and made a mental note to add him to her gratitude list.

"It's just a habit now, I guess. In the last few months when I saw this kitchen light on, I knew that I needed to check on Gladys. She knew this house like the back of her hand, and I know that if she didn't want me to see that she was up, she could well have left the light off. It was like an understood signal – kitchen light on, I come over. I'll try to stop this habit for you. I don't mean to intrude, honestly, I just wanted to make sure you were doing alright."

"I appreciate the concern. I haven't had anyone check on me for many years. Actually, I believe you were the last one who cared enough to check on me regularly. I'd say you were right when you said 'old habit'. Would you like a cup of tea?"

Jonathan made his way to the kitchen table as if it were a daily ritual. "I'd love a cup of tea if it's one of Gladys's special blends," he responded and chuckled

"You know, I used to get so teased by the big wigs at my company for drinking tea while they guzzled coffee. Unfortunately, I could never find any blend that could come close to what Gladys made. I know that woman put special blessings in each batch!" "I'm still praying that she wrote the recipe down some-where and that I can find it. I should probably take a scoop out and decipher it before it's all gone." Sheila felt that pain in her heart again. Mom's tea running out was just another confirmation that her mother was no longer here, in physical form anyway.

"Don't look so sad," Jonathan said, and he reached for Sheila's hand. "You know that she's still around you, right?"

"That's just it. I can't feel her at all. I always thought that once Mom crossed over that I would still be able to connect to her. Maybe I just used that as my way of coping with her aging. I feel so disconnected and lost." Sheila replied.

"You realize your world has been turned upside down, right? I mean, you are used to being the one flying all over the world to someone's rescue. Now, you are here full time, no one to heal, nothing to fix. That's a huge change for you, am I right?"

Sheila didn't respond other than to nod in agreement.

"When was the last time you did your magic?" Jonathan asked. For some reason Sheila was surprised he brought the subject up. In her mind, it was the reason they parted ways so very long ago.

"I'm shocked that you would even broach this subject, Jonathan. I didn't think you agreed with my ways. I don't want this to come between us again, please. Can we just not talk about it?"

"Sheila, I think there is a lot we need to talk about. There are things I need to clear up, things I need to acknowledge about myself and you, us."

Sheila was immediately consumed with guilt. There was a lot she needed to tell him but she just didn't feel it was time. She had to get her feet back under her before she opened another Pandora's box. Their breakup - or break off - had been sudden and harsh as far as she was concerned. Her mind went back over twenty years to that moment under the tree when she just knew that Jonathan was going to propose but instead he came to tell her he was taking a job in the city, leaving that day. He didn't ask her to come with him, he just said he was leaving. She had asked herself a gazillion times why she was so stupid to believe that this college educated guy from down the road was going to be happy living a simple life in the country with her and her magic.

"I know there is a lot we need to talk about, things we should say but not today. Mina called this morning and she's on her way here. I'd like to concentrate on having a wonderful visit with her."

"That's wonderful news. I'm so glad she's coming. I feel that she will be one of the main people who can help you find your footing again, whatever that might be. I'm hoping to meet her again and get to know her too," Jonathan said as he sipped his tea.

"I'm not sure how long she's staying this time but I'd like for you to get to know her too. She's amazing" Sheila said, trying to sound calm as her heart jumped out of her chest. She definitely was not ready for that possibility now.

Jonathan could feel it was time for him to go as the energy in the kitchen had changed from ease and possibilities to confusion and guilt. He just wasn't sure if it was his guilt or Sheila's. One of the things Jonathan longed to share with Sheila was that he had stepped into his own magical gifts; reading energy was one of them. He wanted to share with her why he really bought the property next door and moved back to the county. Didn't she realize that he could live anywhere in the world and he chose next door? Magical women could be so clueless sometimes, he laughed to himself as they said their goodbyes in the early morning.

CHAPTER 19

"**M**om!" Mina yelled as she opened the kitchen door and a worried feeling came over her. Mina expected Sheila to greet her at the driveway as usual, not make her search. "Mom?" Mina called as she was walking through the house. This was more than a house, it was her foundation, her core, her solid base so that she could grow into the woman she was born to be, move to the city and take risks like starting her own business before she was thirty.

Mina passed her room to go to Sheila's bedroom but her mom wasn't in there. Then she heard her mother crying "Please, Momma, please stop. The baby is still crying. Mom, please stop that lady! She's making the baby cry!"

Mina rushed to Meme's room where she found Sheila curled up in the fetal position crying in her sleep. "Mom, Mom" Mina gently shook Sheila trying to wake her easily from the torment she was obviously experiencing in this dream. "Mom"

Sheila woke up startled that Mina was there already. She had just lain down a couple of minutes ago to help fight the fatigue from so many restless nights in a row.

"Mina, I'm so glad you are here!" Sheila wrapped her arms around her daughter, trying to fill herself with present love and comfort which was way different from the dream state she had just left.

"Mom, are you okay?"

"Oh, yes, Mina. I'm fine. I was in Meme's room just reminiscing, trying to feel some sort of connection to her. I just miss her and at times it feels overwhelming. But, that's grief for you, no explanation for the waves of sadness, happiness, loneliness and love you feel all at once."

Sheila tried to put on a comforting smile. "I know Mom, I feel the same stuff. It means that we loved her deeply. But I'm more concerned with the dream you were having."

"I'm chalking it up to the shadow work I need to do in order to move forward."

"Ok, Mom, let's do what Meme would tells us we needed – grow our roots!" Mina grabbed Sheila's hand and they walked outside.

As they walked hand in hand to the corner of the yard, they both knew where they were going without even talking about it. They were headed to "The Tree". This tree was infamous to the family. This tree had witnessed happiness, love, heartbreak, gratitude, anger and everything else this lineage had experienced on this property. This tree healed the hurt, eased the pain, danced in the wind to rejoice in celebration. Where else would they go to "grow their roots"? They found a place near the base of the tree and sat cross-legged in the grass, feeling the coolness of the shade.

"Meme taught me long ago that grounding into Mother Earth is essential to a balanced life. She used to say that all I had to do was imagine that I was sitting under this tree. Then, let her branches protect me from the world and my roots sunk deep into the earth, to the core of her light. Once I felt it, let that light come back up through my roots into my feet, working its way up through my body and out the top of my head. This light was what connects us to Spirit, filling us with light, strength and love. I try to do this at least every morning and have found if I do it for at least ten seconds several times a day, I'm so much more centered and don't seem to react to chaos. And as simple as this part of the prayer work is, it is the easiest one for me to forget to do" Mina chuckled.

"You? I've been looking at this tree for a few weeks, and I haven't remembered to ground," Sheila said shaking her head at herself.

The girls spent the next several minutes in silence grounding themselves into Mother Earth, connecting to her core light, feeling that light come back up through their roots filling them with bright light – up through their feet, their knees, their hips, their sacral chakras, up through their cores, their hearts, throats, behind their eyes, and out the top of their heads. They then saw the light go high into the air, a hole opening in the clouds where the light of God met with their light from Mother Earth. They saw this light get brighter and stronger as the energies from above and below met, filling them with God's love and light. Individually, they encompassed themselves in the energy ball then expanded it out to the entire land, their county, their state, their country and the world ending with their energetic arms wrapped around Mother Earth in a hug of gratitude and thanks.

The two ladies simultaneously opened their eyes, smiling at each other, feeling so calm and peaceful.

"How's that, Mom?"

"Mina, that was an answer to several prayers, I must say."

"Tell me about this dream you keep having. Maybe together we can figure it out and ease this pain."

"Oh, you know how dreams go sometimes. It's that I just hear a crying baby. I was feeling so much grief. I'm just thinking that the grief of losing Mom is triggering the grief of leaving you. I think it's me reliving the heartbreak of having to go away. I mean, I know I chose it, though it didn't feel like I had a choice. I kept telling myself that I was doing this so that you wouldn't have to leave your family, your child. It's just shadow work that I need to do but it didn't feel I had my feet under me yet from the loss of Mom."

"I know I was really hard on you for leaving me. I blamed you for everything. I have apologized for that and I really mean it. I put my feelings of separation from this place and Meme all on you and I'm the one who left. From the bottom of my heart, Mom, I do not in any way, shape, or form have any hate, anger or grief towards you. Please know that there is no reason for you to continue to be consumed with sorrow for the years we missed together. Looking back, I knew - know - that your energy was always with me. Meme told me stories about you every single day. You were my imaginary friend. As far as I'm concerned, we are better than good. Don't you feel the same?" Mina asked almost afraid her mom didn't share the healing and connection.

"I absolutely do feel the same Mina. That's why this is so weird."

"Tell me about the dream this morning" Mina said as she reached for Sheila's hand to comfort and support her mother.

Sheila took a deep breath as she considered just brushing the nightmare off again but this heartbreak was seeping into her waking state. "Okay, but you know that dreams don't always follow an easy storyline so hang on. This might get complicated." The girls got to their feet to stroll the property. "At first it seems that I am about twenty something and I'm looking at the door ready to leave but a baby keeps crying. I can hear myself begging Mom to please, please comfort you or I'm not leaving. Then I'm about three and I see Mom watching a lady try to comfort a baby, not you, but the baby won't stop crying. I am again begging mom to please take the baby in her arms so she will stop crying. Then I am standing at the Tree and I'm begging myself to stop crying. See, it's just so confusing."

"Ok, how did you feel when you woke up?" Mina asked.

"Grief, sorrow and deep, deep sadness was the overwhelming and theme," Sheila said was a tear streaked down her cheek.

"Are there any specific colors that seem to run through the dream?" Mina continued with the questions.

"Green! I didn't realize until you asked me but green stands out. I'm in a green dress when I'm leaving you, I'm in a green dress when I'm a child and I'm in a green dress sobbing under the tree."

"Well, green does represent a positive change, hope and peace. Maybe, Dream Source is trying to relay to you that even though it seemed like the grief was overwhelming at the time, the best outcome possible would happen through the tears. How does that feel?"

"That feels right. I mean, you did turn out pretty damn awesome thanks to Meme." Sheila smiled.

"Ok, so how does that translate to the other two instances?"

Sheila shrugging her shoulders, replied "I'm not sure yet, but I definitely feel like this is a path of questions I can take back into the dream state by asking right before going to sleep." Sheila actually felt lighter and more optimistic than she had in days.

CHAPTER 20

After the stroll and dream consultation between mother and daughter, the two ladies found themselves back at the kitchen table.

"How about a cup of tea?" Sheila asked as she rose to turn the stove on for the teapot of water.

"Is it Meme's special blend?"

"Nothing but the best for my amazing daughter." Sheila smiled over her shoulder.

"Looks like you are getting a bit low. Do you have more stashed? Or do you have a recipe?"

"You know, this is the last I have of her tea. That makes me so sad. I'm planning on searching this place hoping to find where she wrote it down." Sheila promised.

"Do you remember that making tea is one of Ellie's specialties?" Mina asked and jumped out of her chair when Sheila dropped the teacup on the counter. "Mom? Are you ok?"

Sheila looked at Mina stunned. "I think so. I had

the same whoosh of grief and sorrow as my dream when you said Eleanor's name. It could the part of my dream where I'm a young girl begging Mom to comfort the crying baby. How weird is that?" Sheila questioned herself as well as Mina. "I'm going to have to sit with that one a bit to dig into the energy connecting the two" Sheila replied, trying to brush off the feelings as she brought the tea servings to the table.

Just then, a knock on the door startled them both. Instant comfort washed over them both before they even answered the door.

"Jonathan," Sheila said without realizing she said it out loud and was smiling. Mina noticed the look on her mom's face and the ease of energy she shifted into. "Come in, Jonathan" Sheila waved from the table. "Would you like some tea?"

"Oh, am I interrupting you two?"

Sheila immediately got nervous when she remembered that Mina was sitting there too. How did she forget that her daughter was sitting at the same table? Somehow Sheila's mind had the two cups set out for herself and Jonathan. Oh geeze, this might get a bit uncomfortable. "Play it cool," Sheila said to herself realizing she had already invited him in and that saying he was interrupting at this point would be extremely rude.

"No, you are not interrupting us. Please come in and join the tea party." Mina said with a cheesy grin. She wanted to learn more about the man her mother seemed to be spending a lot more time with.

Jonathan was happier than he had been in years as he sat down. He was good at reading energy but this was off the charts. The three of them in the same house, the same room, was what he had dreamed of.

"You know, Gladys and I spent many hours at this table over the last year. That woman had the best stories that went along with the best tea in the land. I feel like I know you already, Mina. How are things in the city?"

"Really good now," Mina said.

"Your Meme told me that you were considering starting your own business. She was so proud of you. You know, she was never happier than when she told me that your and your mom were spending time together. She said she had done a lot of prayer work to make that happen," Jonathan chuckled.

For some reason it didn't surprise Mina that Jonathan knew about that, and fortunately he was kind enough not to bring up the subject of Brock. "Sounds like you and Meme shared a bunch. I'd love to hear the stories Meme passed on to you. She was a great storyteller."

"And so knowledgeable," Jonathan added. "She was full of magic. There was a purpose and intent to every single thing she did. She had regrets too, though. I think we all do on some level."

"Mom had regrets?" Sheila finally spoke up. "About what?"

Jonathan realized he shouldn't have started down this road with these two. He remembered that it was hard to get much past Sheila and suspected that Mina was more difficult to get by than her mother.

"Oh, you know, we all have regrets. I don't want to divulge anything that was told to me in confidence." Jonathan tried to skirt this question.

"Saved by the bell," Mina said as her cell phone rang. It was one of her new clients and she didn't want to risk a negative impression this early in the game. "Excuse me, please, I have to take this call from a new client," Mina said as she got up from the kitchen table.

Mina was right, Jonathan thought, he was saved by that bell and acknowledged that his powers were getting better as he had said a prayer for that ringer to go off.

Mina came back to the table with a frown on her face, "I'm so very sorry, Mom, but I have to go back to the city. This new client has an emergency and wants me by her side."

"That's what forming a business relationship is all about in the beginning, holding their hands through every "seeming" emergency" Jonathan replied.

Mina looked shocked as she didn't realize that he was a businessman. She just thought he was the guy down the road. "I'm sorry, Jonathan, to cut out on our conversations. I feel like there is so much I can learn from you," Mina said as she reached out to give him a hug.

"Let me get take your bag to the car while you say your 'see ya laters' to your mom" Jonathan offered.

Mina had forgotten she left her bag by the door when she got there. "Oh, thank you. I really appreciate it," Mina said. Jonathan quietly slipped out the door as Mina walked to her mom's side "Mom, are you sure you are ok? I can come back first thing in the morning."

"I'm fine. Actually, I'm better than this morning. I can't thank you enough for running to my side to help me grow my roots." They both laughed at the phrase Meme had stuck in their heads. "I have some deep diving to do into my thoughts, my beliefs, before I can move forward. You have definitely helped me get on the path to doing that."

"I would not be leaving you if you didn't have support here." Mina pointed over her shoulder, where Jonathan was putting her overnight bag in the car.

Sheila blushed "He's an old friend and has been a ton of comfort knowing he's down the road should I need anything."

"Okay, Mom, whatever you say." Mina laughed and hugged her mom goodbye. "Love you," they exchanged as Mina walked out the door.

Mina walked to her car smiling, at Jonathan and grateful that they had a couple of minutes together alone. Jonathan had this energy about him that Mina couldn't put her finger on. She felt so comfortable with him, almost like she had known him for years. It was like he made her feel safe, but how in the world could that be? This was only the second time she had seen him in person. She was questioning her memory to see if her mom or her grandmother had ever mentioned that name. At that moment, she couldn't find the connection but somehow knew that there was one, a deep one.

"Mina, have a safe trip. Here's my cell number if you ever need anything." Jonathan handed Mina his business card with a questioning look. "You know, like if you can't get in touch with your mom or you need me to check on her or anything" Jonathan answered the question that Mina hadn't even asked.

"Thank you! Really, thank you. I feel so much better about Mom being here alone with you just down the road." With that, they exchanged a friendly hug and Mina hopped in her car to head back to the city.

Jonathan headed back to the kitchen where he found Sheila at the table deep in thought. "Did Mina help you with your nightmare?" Jonathan asked.

"How did you know that's what I was thinking about?" Sheila asked.

"For one, it's written all over your face."

"And for two?" Sheila asked again.

"Sheila, there's a lot I need to tell you, explain to you. I didn't realize it until I saw the two of you at the kitchen table but I feel like this will help you with your dream."

Sheila started to get up from the table. She wasn't ready for this conversation with Jonathan. She wasn't ready for this much truth to come out. She knew she had to tell him but this wasn't the way she had planned.

Jonathan reached for her hand "Please, let me talk. You don't have to say a word." Sheila slowly sat back down, looking at Jonathan in the eyes.

While he still had her hand in his, Jonathan took a deep breath and began his side of their story "That day under the tree when I made the biggest mistake in my life wasn't what I had planned. I don't know if you realize it or not but I had a ring in my pocket for you."

Sheila's mouth dropped open, as her ears couldn't believe what he was saying.

"My full intention while walking to meet you was to get on one knee and beg you to marry me. With each step, that plan faded. All the calls and letters I was getting from big companies all over the country kept coming in my head. I knew that I wanted to marry you and take you with me. I couldn't imagine a life without you. I also knew how selfish I was being and that I loved you too much to even suggest you leave your truth to follow my path. What you thought was our biggest hurdle was your beliefs. What you didn't know was that my own magic had become stronger and stronger. I wanted so much to talk to you about it but I wasn't sure how I felt."

Sheila, now shocked and puzzled could only ask "Your magic?"

"Yes. I had started in college, secretly inspired by you and the letters you would send me while I was away. I would set my intention for something to happen, and it would. It happened exactly how I saw it. So, I started playing with it more and more, like this paper would get an A, and the score of the football game was exactly as I said it would be. I would write down that I had received a letter from a firm and within a week I would receive a letter! I was amazed. I started solidifying stocks' rise and fall, no, not a lot, but enough to make an impression on big-city firms. They thought my predictions were just luck. I had built a nice nest for the two of us and created the offer from the firm I desired. What I was doing was being my magic, my bigness. I couldn't wait to share this with you. With each step towards that tree, I realized that I would be asking you to leave your magic, your path for mine. I loved you too much to do that."

All Sheila could ask was, "So what brought you back here? You can't say it was me because I was still traveling when you moved back"

"I had done everything I could think of to fill the void of you. No matter who I dated, their energy was not match for yours. No matter how many big deals I closed, no matter how much money I made, the void was still there. I was burned out. I was done with that life. Then, as if I had scripted it, which I didn't consciously anyway, I got a call to inform me that the property was for sale, and I was asked to help. I knew in my heart that I was being called back to this place. So, I came back and met with the owner to work out the details. Once the offer was agreed on, I resigned and moved back home. I've been trying to fix the place up since. The best part was getting to know Gladys on a deeper level. We shared so much, and I came to love her like a mother. She had given me permission to check on her energetically any time, as well as to come to the kitchen whenever I felt called. In the last few months of her life, we had a routine. We would have tea mid-morning that came with a story. Sheila, Meme had regrets. I hate to say it, but she did. She finally admitted to me that she was the one who had done her magic to stop me from proposing to you that day. She was so afraid of you leaving that she could not see a future without you here. She knew you had great abilities to heal, but she never thought you would be traveling the world practicing. She was sorry from the moment I left. She tried so hard to make it up to you."

"Wait, WHAT? Mom stopped you from proposing? How could she do that? Why didn't she tell me? Especially after I found out I was pregnant with Mina?" Sheila instantly covered her mouth gasping.

Damn it! That wasn't the way she wanted to tell him. Sheila started crying, sobbing actually. It was the same sob from the dream, but it wasn't grief - it was overwhelming abandonment. "I'm sorry I didn't tell you sooner. I wanted to but to see you at Mom's funeral kind of took me by surprise. Mom had mentioned here and there that you were in the area but I didn't quite put two and two together that you had moved back permanently."

"It's okay. I already knew that Mina was mine. Oh, not then. I would not have left if I'd known you were pregnant. Gladys finally admitted it to me in one of our conversations. Every time she would tell me about something Mina had done, I felt this amazing connection to her. It was like I could see and feel her energy as a baby, a child and as an adult. I felt pride, sorrow, happiness, horror when Gladys would talk about Mina, just like I assumed a parent would. One day I actually asked Gladys, and she told me the whole story."

"Well, at least that's off my chest. I've been trying to find the right time and place to talk to you about this. I'm glad we've cleared the air about everything. I've so enjoyed your company the last several weeks. Now with this out in the open, I can better appreciate our time together." Sheila said.

"Well, there are a couple more things we need to

talk about, Sheila. I take it you haven't told Mina yet." Sheila shook her head no in response but did not say a word. "Let's do it together, shall we?" Jonathan asked.

Sheila only nodded, this time it was yes. She was exhausted, and her head was spinning from all the information, the lack of sleep and the magic she and Mina had done that morning. Jonathan could read Sheila's energy and gently helped her to stand then guided her back to her own bedroom where she could get some rest. Once she had settled, he placed a quilt over her and quietly left. He knew she needed time alone, as well as some deep sleep. As Sheila drifted off to sleep, she realized she was wearing a green dress just like in the nightmare under the tree.

CHAPTER 21

Sheila had just woken up from the deepest most peaceful sleep she had had in weeks. Even though the nap was only a couple of hours, she felt more rested and full of energy. She decided as she put a pot of water on for tea that now was the time to start digging for the famous Gladys tea recipe. Sheila knew there were a couple of places her mom kept secret stuff, so she headed to her mom's bedroom to start her search. Sheila first went to the top drawer of her mother's chest. She could remember as a kid looking up at that drawer and imagining all the magical stuff her mom hid in there. However, after rummaging through the top drawer she came up empty-handed. There wasn't much in there other than an old picture of her mom holding a baby as Sheila stood next to them both smiling.

Sheila then headed to the nightstand next to the bed. That drawer was hard to open because it was stuffed full of papers. She couldn't imagine what was so important in those documents that her mother couldn't through away. As Sheila yanked the draw open, several envelopes flew out of it. She assumed the envelopes from the bank were her mother's checking account statements, but that's not what she found when she opened one of the letters. As Sheila read in horror and confusion, the bank was recalling the mortgage due to non-payment and gave a deadline of less than a year ago. This made no sense because her Mom had told her that she left the land to the two of us. How could Mom leave the place to her and Mina if they recalled the note? How could she have taken her last breath if the bank had recalled the note? Gladys had even told her that there was more than enough money to take care of the place for years to come and there would be no worries on the financial front. How could this be? One day the bank is going to take the only home you have ever lived in, and the next it's all good? Sheila knew she had to call Jonathan because he was the only one business-savvy enough to explain this to her.

As if she had already called him, Jonathan was at the kitchen door when she walked out of the bedroom. "How are you feeling? Did the nap help?" he asked.

"Well, I'm not sure now. I thought I felt better so I started looking for the tea recipe. I was going through some of mom's paperwork and found a letter from the bank. Can you help me figure this out?

I mean, one day she's getting letters that say they are going to sell her home out from underneath her, and the next she has hundreds of thousands of dollars in her bank account. What does this mean? She told me she left the house to the two of us, me and Mina, and said there was nothing to worry about financially. How can that be if they were going to foreclose on her days before?"

"Sheila, please sit down. I'll fix the tea. I take it you haven't seen a copy of Gladys's will yet?"

Sheila shook her head in response. Seems like she had limited words when it came to responding to Jonathan's questions today.

Jonathan started again with a deep breath: "I was going to go into this earlier but your energy felt like it had had all you could handle at that time. Remember when I said I got a call about the property being for sale?"

"Yes, you mean your family's property?"

"Well, yes and no. I did purchase my family's home several years ago when the deep drought came through and killed all the crops and most of the live-stock. Many of the families around had trouble, and I did all I could to help the entire community. Your mother was stubborn as she refused any help from anyone. She swore she would make it on her own. About a year ago, I got a call from the bank. Matt, the bank president, and I went to school together and had worked on the deal to help the community the first time. The banker loved your mother and hated what was happening to her. He said it broke his heart each time he had to sign the letters going out to her for payment. Everyone in that bank tried all they could to help Gladys, but being full of pride, she refused. They tried getting in touch with you, but your contact information was the same as hers."

"So, that's the call you got confirming it was time for you to return?" Sheila asked.

"Yes, but Gladys did not make it that easy. I came to meet with her and offered to give her the money and she absolutely refused. Knowing how stubborn and full of pride she was, I offered to just loan her the money, and that didn't work either. Finally, after a multitude of conversations over cups of hot tea, I came up with a business plan where we could sell her tea leaves and I'd back the business financially, provide all of the marketing, order processing, packaging and mailing. She said she'd have to think about it. Over the next couple of days, I would come by and pretty much beg her to take the deal. It was the most difficult negotiations of my life.

Finally she agreed to let me back her business and I wrote her a check. We started making a plan to fix up the place so that it could support her business. I promised to be very hands-on and that's what I did. I made every repair to the best of my abilities and only called in help with the projects that were over my head, like electricity and HVAC. I never left her alone when there was a stranger on the place. After they left, we would sprinkle blessed salt around the perimeters and doors to secure her safety." Jonathan winked at Sheila with that last sentence because they both new how much the little things like that meant to Gladys.

"So, you have the tea recipe? I've been talking about it for days and yet you have it?"

"No" he replied "I do not. Gladys never got around to giving it to me. I actually never brought it up, and I didn't think she really had it written down or could remember the ingredients. I knew she was ill when I came back and I was just hoping to give her some comfort in her last months. She kept saying her daughter was the tea maker in the family. I thought you had created it and was just pulling my leg this whole time."

"I don't know anything about the ingredients to her tea. Actually, when I'm working with a client I reach out to a dear friend in the city. She always seems to have just the right tea for whatever my clients are dealing with. She's the master as far as I'm concerned."

At the very moment Sheila thought of Eleanor, that same overwhelming feeling of abandonment consumed her. So much so that she could barely hold in a sob that was coming from deep inside her. She managed to hold in the sob but not the tear rolling down her cheek.

Jonathan wiped the tear away, "What's wrong? Where is that horrific sadness coming from, Sheila?"

"I don't know," Sheila replied. "It's that same feeling I have when I wake up from the dream. After spending time with Mina this morning I have come to realize that it's not grief that I'm feeling, it's abandonment. I felt it when you left me under the Tree, and I felt it when I left Mina with Mom to go be with my first out-of-town client. What I can't put my finger on is what would make the three-year-old me feel abandoned. Leana. Do you now a Leana? Have you heard that name before? It's just now coming to me. The young me is asking my mom about Leana."

"You know, your mom did call you Leana a couple of times when we were talking, but I thought she was just getting confused because she was tired or not feeling well. She did not elaborate on the name or any connection." Jonathan said.

Sheila shrugged the reference off pretty much just like her mother had months before. Her head was once again spinning with all the new information Jonathan had shared. What in the hell was she going to do now? She didn't have the money to pay Jonathan back for a business that didn't even exist. Why didn't she realize that her own mother was in that bad of financial shape? Had it really been that long since she had been home and seen the disrepair herself?

Reading her thoughts, Jonathan replied, "You know she didn't want you to take on the burden of this place. She knew you loved traveling and helping others. She only wanted you to come back her if and when you felt it right. She wanted life on her terms, and she hoped that for you too. She regretted stepping in between us before and was determined to not meddle in our lives again."

Jonathan put an arm around Sheila to offer some sort of comfort and support. Instantly Sheila melted in his embrace and laid her head on his shoulder. This felt so good, so right, so comfortable, but then she jolted upright stiff as a board. She had too much information and planning to get through to add this to her emotional plate.

"I need to think now."

"Okay, I'm heading home. Let me know if you

need anything, no matter what time it is. Promise?" he asked and left when she nodded in response.

After sitting at the table with her mind running wild, she reached for her cell phone to call Mina. Mina actually answered before Sheila had time to hang up.

"Mina, I just wanted to check on you and make sure everything was okay."

Mina knew instantly that something was wrong because her mother did not just call to check on her.

"Mom, what's going on? What's wrong?"

"Oh, nothing really" Sheila couldn't hold it in any longer and broke down in tears.

"There's so much going on, so much information I learned today."

"Okay, I'll be there in a couple of hours. I'm turning the car onto the highway now. Why don't you go take a hot salt bath and call me when you get out? I love you."

Sheila hung up the phone and did what she was told. A long hot bath would do wonders. Mina, on the other hand, made one more call before she left the city. If anyone knew what to give her mother to soothe her nerves and nightmares, it would be Ellie.

CHAPTER 22

S heila was in the hot tub for what seemed like hours. It was amazing what the Spirits of Water, Lavender, and Salt could do for one's mind and body as the tension and stress left her entire energy. Although she felt clearer, Sheila knew she had to be strong for Mina. There would be a lot of information given to her tonight that could change her world. Sheila did her prayer work that this would all be easier than she ever imagined possible. Sheila heard a knock at the door as she was heading to the kitchen. Of course, it was Jonathan with a basket of food.

"I thought you might need some food. I wasn't sure if you had even eaten today."

"You know, I can't even remember" Sheila laughed as she took the basket from his arms and spread the meal out on the table.

Jonathan grabbed plates from the cupboard and utensils from the drawers just like it was an ordinary thing that they were sharing a meal he had prepared.

As they sat down to eat, Sheila said, "Wow, I didn't know you could cook like this."

Jonathan just shrugged "What else was I supposed to do with all that time on my hands?"

"It looks and smells amazing," Sheila said as she started scarfing down the delicious food.

"I think I brought enough for Mina too. Do you know what time she will be in tonight?" Jonathan asked.

Sheila stopped chewing and swallowed hard. "I didn't tell you she was coming tonight."

"I know you didn't verbally tell me, but I knew when I left you would call her and she would be back. Have you not yet figured out that I'm intuitive too?"

"That's going to take some getting used to, for sure," Sheila said and took another big bite. She hadn't realized she was so hungry. This was definite confirmation that big energy had moved in her and she would be finding her footing soon.

Before she could take another bite the door flung open.

"Mom! Are you -- I was going to ask if you were okay, but I see that the salt bath did you a world of good. I guess I can go back home if I'm interrupting something," Mina said when she saw the nice dinner on the table and the two of them seemingly enjoying each other's company.

Jonathan jumped up and pulled out a chair. "Mina, it's good to see you again today. Please join us. I made enough for all of us."

Mina looked at her mother and back at Jonathan. "Is this a set-up or something? Mom, you sounded awful on the phone."

"I know Mina. I have a lot to tell you, and it just can't wait any longer. Plus, I need your help, business sense."

"You have the best businessman in the world right here at your kitchen table. Do you know who this man is? Do you know the things he has done in the business world? I knew you looked familiar, but when I saw your business card, it finally clicked who you were. I studied you in college. You are a marvel at business. I can't imagine why you two would need me."

"Well, Mina, I don't know about all his business stuff but I do know the guy I grew up with and am learning about the man he is today," Sheila replied.

Mina sat down at the table as Jonathan got a place setting for her. "I can leave the two of you alone now as I know you have a lot to discuss. I can come back and clean up in the morning."

"Please stay" Sheila asked. "You are a big part of this discussion."

It was Sheila who took a deep breath this time before starting the story, "Mina, this afternoon after you left, I felt so drained I took a peaceful, restful nap. When I got up, I decided to look for Meme's tea recipe. I when I pulled out the drawer to her nightstand a bunch of letters came flying out. They were letters from the bank demanding payment on the place or they were going to foreclose. I was so confused because she told me that the property was to go to the two of us. I also knew that there was plenty of money in the bank, so how did she go from foreclosure to wealth in merely months? That's when Jonathan filled in the gaps.

Sheila filled her daughter in on Meme's bank troubles. "It seems that a few years ago, Jonathan helped the community to recover. Matt, the bank president, had called Jonathan after several attempts to help Mom with the note. Mother, being her stubborn self, would not refinance or consider any help whatsoever on the farm. Jonathan came back and offered her the money outright. She refused, as well as firmly declining when he offered to loan her the money. Long story short, Jonathan finally convinced her to let him back a tea business."

"A what?" Mina asked.

Jonathan chimed in, "I was trying to find some way for her to let me help. We came up with the thought of building a business with her famous tea recipe. Honestly, she would only do it on one condition."

"And that one condition was that Jonathan work with her and no one else. She was trying to make amends, Mina," Sheila continued. It was now or never, so she went on "Remember Jonathan said that Meme had regrets? I didn't realize this either, but Meme was trying to make amends. Many years ago, Jonathan and I were in love. We were high school sweethearts and even made it through his college years. He was on his way to propose to me, and Meme got scared I would leave her and the family business. So, she did her powerful prayer work and –"

Jonathan interrupted, "And by the time I got to that tree out there with the ring in my pocket, I had changed my mind. I was going to make a name for myself and come back for her. I couldn't ask her to follow my dream and leave hers behind. I loved her too much to ask that of her. What neither of us realized yet was that she was pregnant with you."

"I knew how successful he had become in a very short time, and I didn't want to bog him down. In my mind, he left me, so I wasn't going to beg him to come back just for a baby. Meme told me we could do it on our own. She said she wasn't going to let another child out of her home again."

Mina's head was spinning. "You mean not only are you some wealthy business guru with companies all over the world, you are my father? I knew we had a connection, but I just thought it was our shared love of business. I mean, when I was studying you in school it was like I could feel your energy around me. Like I knew what move you were going to make to close those big deals. And, then seeing you at Meme's funeral, I felt this weird comfort around you. Then today I felt it again, but once I got your business card, I just brushed it off to the college days."

"Mina, are you ok? I'm sorry I didn't tell either one of you the truth. I should have years ago" Sheila said.

"But when did you find out?" Mina asked Jonathan.

"Actually, I only found out at the funeral. By that I mean I instantly instinctively knew as no one had said the words until your mother did this morning."

"Hell of a secret you kept there, Mom. I can say one thing though. You never lied about it. I don't ever remember questioning why I didn't have a father around or if I even had one. So, what do we do now, just become this one big happy family?" Mina shot out a bit sarcastically.

"Actually, that's why I called you Mina. I know you have what I'm coming to understand as your father's business sense. I want to come up with a way we can pay Jonathan back. This is probably the only business contract where he lost money. So how do we do that?" Sheila asked.

"Hold up! I made this deal knowing full well that I would not see one cent, nor do I plan on it now. I have already claimed the loss and am moving ahead. It's a done deal in my book," Jonathan explained.

"Can he do that Mina?"

"Of course he can do that. He can pretty much do whatever he wants. Big companies need tax write-offs too," Mina said.

"But what if we did find Mom's recipe and sell the tea leaves? Can't we still do that?" Sheila was trying hard to find a way to pay Jonathan back so that she didn't feel obligated to his money.

"The first thing you need is the recipe. I can attest to the fact that I have yet to come across that exact blend anywhere in the world," Jonathan reminded the ladies.

"That reminds me, Mina, today after you left, I remember part of my dream either saying or hearing the name Leana. Have you ever heard Meme say that name? I think Leana"

A big crash sounded as a jar of tea leaves hit the floor. Eleanor had just walked in to surprise her two dear friends. Mina had stopped by the shop, asking for her suggestions on what to bring Sheila to ease her grief and help her work through the nightmares.

All three of them turned and stared at Ellie as she whispered, "I haven't heard that name in years. No one has called me that since I was a baby. I don't even know why I remember that."

"You're Leana?" Sheila asked.

"I think I am," she replied. A wave of immeasurable sadness and grief filled the air as well as the energy of both Sheila and Ellie. The exact same abandonment feeling that filled the nightmare for Sheila. What did all this mean? How did Ellie fit into the crying baby Sheila was so upset over in the dream? Ellie was just a little girl who had grown up at the other end of the county. Sheila didn't really know her until Ellie got sick and asked for Sheila's help healing.

Mina rushed to Ellie as Jonathan rushed to Sheila, helping both ladies to the kitchen table. Once they were seated, Jonathan asked to be excused. Sheila was afraid he was leaving this whole mess wanting nothing to do with the drama, the magic or the family.

"I'll be right back. I have something that may give us some answers." With that, he swiftly left the kitchen while the other three sat trying to comfort each other. This was something out of a freaking story book. This shit didn't happen in real life, Mina just knew it. She was still having trouble wrapping her head around the fact that the world's foremost business guru was actually her father. Now, he's backed a business with her Meme to sell her tea leaves that we don't have a recipe for, and now Ellie is Leana? Who the hell is Leana? She needed a glass of wine and was sure they did too.

"Eleanor, what else do you remember from your childhood?" Sheila asked.

"Really not much other than being called Leana, then Ellie. I used my full name once I moved to the city in a way to separate me from the county. I remember not feeling like I belonged anywhere while growing up. I know that most women who have abilities feel like the black sheep of their families, but this was different. I always wondered why there was no real bond between me and my mother. She always felt like more of an aunt to me. Don't get me wrong, she was motherly, cared and provided for me, but there was no bond. I always thought I was just missing something or that this is what all other girls felt with their mothers and yet still felt the void," Ellie replied.

At that moment, Jonathan reappeared with a white sealed envelope in his hand. "I had actually forgotten that Gladys had given me this as part of our business deal. I was not to open it until she had passed. I had to promise to give it to you, Sheila at a time after the funeral that I felt appropriate. I'd say this was appropriate, wouldn't you agree?"

The other three nodded in unison. Jonathan open the sealed envelope and began reading what would appear to be a handwritten note or will of some sort." "Ladies, if you are reading this, I have crossed over. I've been there a time or two for an instant, and if it's anything like what I witnessed, then trust that I am in a great spot and will continue to watch over you. Know that I am extremely proud of you all. I have watched your grow from my arms into amazing women. I have done some things that I regret. I would like to explain the circumstances around my decisions that have and will affect your lives.

"When I was married to the love of my life for

less than six years, the unforeseen happened that changed this family's trajectory. Your father and I were in a horrible accident in which he lost his life. I wasn't expected to live, either. Fortunately, I barely pulled through with a very long healing process. It became impossible for me to take care of both of my girls, and one of the amazing ladies caring for me was having trouble conceiving. The community convinced me that it would be in the best interest for both girls if she were to help raise the youngest. It was the hardest decision I ever had to make and live with. I tried to be a loving mother to one while grieving the other and hating myself for the hand I had been dealt. I tried so hard to support baby Leana from afar as I was not allowed to see her or hold her during her youth.

"Once Sheila had begun her healing path and allowed me to help with baby Mina, my heart was soothed some, but not completely. I found out that Leana had moved to the city and owned a very successful retail store. Once Leana fell ill, I had to help. I sent money through the community to support the store until Leana could get back on her feet. I did my very best to support you all. However, I failed terribly. While trying to support the store, a historical drought swept the land. Neighbors and friends lost almost everything. That is, until a businessman filled the local bank with money so that loans could be made, interest-free I might add, and the community saved.

"Legend has it that not one dime was collected on any of those loans. That, however, you will have to ask that business-man, right, Jonathan? I managed to hold on as long as I could. I was not going to take a loan from anyone. This community had already helped me once after my beloved passed away. I swore never to put my community at risk again by asking for help. Jonathan came to meet me one day and offered me a loan. Of course, I declined the generous offer. I wasn't going to leave my girls with a debt so big they would never recover. Besides, I already felt so guilty for the spell I had placed on Jonathan so many years ago that again harmed my family with good intentions. Finally, Jonathan and I came to a deal, we were going into business together. Mind you, this was only after he convinced me that he was the answer to my money prayer work. I promised to sell my tea recipe to him and he would run the business, at least until the investment had been profitable.

"I never did remember where I put that recipe. It didn't really belong to me anyway. It was one I had ordered time and time again from Leana's shop. One of her amazing talents is tea medicine. My hope is that finally I can help my family by bringing them together rather than tearing them apart. Therefore, I leave the property to my two girls, Sheila and Leana, with the understanding that should they decide to sell before they pass that my beautiful Mina gets first chance. I pray that you can somehow find it in your hearts to forgive me for my short sightedness and find your way back to each other as sisters. I pray that Sheila and Jonathan can forgive my fears and interference and find their way back to each other. I pray that you all learn from my meddling mistakes and learn to lean on each other through this process. I truly love you all, Mom, Meme, Gladys," Jonathan ended by folding the letter.

All three women were in complete shock. None of them could have imagined all that had transpired in their young lives. Sheila knew her dad had been killed in an accident, but she had no idea that her mother was almost killed as well. She also had no idea she had a sister, especially a person she already knew and loved. Eleanor had no idea that any of this was possible, to have a sister and a niece that she already adored like her own family. Well, duh, they were family! One thing was for sure as they all four sat around that kitchen table, none of them felt resentment towards Gladys. They only felt love, understanding, and mostly clarity for all that had transpired that day. No one had anything to say as they all sat there drinking the wine that thankfully Mina had poured earlier.

Finally, Jonathan broke the silence, raised his glass and said, "Well, ladies, here's to family."

After everything that had just happened, they could only chuckle as they raised their glasses and said in unison, "Family!"

ABOUT THE AUTHOR

Kimberly Tobin is the creator and owner of Mystic CEO, an author, speaker, change mentor, and business strategist helping spiritual women clearly acknowledge and embrace their unique gifts that fears often conceal. She is passionate about helping women see that even the smallest of prayers and the simplest of rituals can celebrate their divine inner magic, helping them become the creators of their lives, not just bystanders. Kimberly has an MBA and over twenty years of accounting and human resources experience in the corporate world, bringing her own creativity to hiring processes and finding the right fit that benefits the employees and the companies. She lives on a small farm in eastern Missouri with her husband, three dogs, and two horses. She works virtually with her clients, offering transformational programs and classes. Kimberly hosts retreats at beautiful locations around the world, where she shares how to weave magic into the mundane, simple and powerful alchemy.

You can follow Kimberly on these social media outlets:

https://www.facebook.com/Mystical.CEO/

https://www.instagram.com/mystical.ceo/

https://twitter.com/Clarity_Kim

Learn more about Kimberly at www.KimberlyTobin. com and download her gift: "Through Fear to Fabulous–Learning to be You." On her website, you will find a plethora of content in her articles, podcasts, and videos at no charge. You can also find more about the programs and retreats she is currently offering.

REVIEWS

"The Legacy, Witches of Greene County is such a fun and enlightening read, I didn't want it to end! Kimberly Tobin weaves real magical practices into a compelling story of a gifted family. I enjoyed getting to know these characters and learning how they use their magic and spiritual gifts in daily practice. It made me very aware of how I use my own magic. I can't wait for Vol. 2!"

~Lynde Thames, Energy Healer
Facebook: Lynde Thames: Intuitive Energy Arts & Healing

"What a great read about family secrets, relationships and the discovery of spirituality within the self. Mina's story of awakening and self-understanding and her complicated relationship with her mother is not only poignant and intriguing, but also relatable on so many levels."

~Aeriol Ascher, Empowerment Leader
www.healingbodymindandsoul.com

"**In The Legacy, Kim Tobin shares a compelling, fictional tale of a family who possess spiritual healing gifts as they reconcile their birthright to love wholely with the challenges of their misunderstood actions. We follow Mina as she leaves her abusive husband and finds her mother who abandoned her in childhood, and discovers they both share the same 'hunches, prayers, angels, guides, God, Spirit, intuition, imagination, seeing and knowing things that others hadn't.' Read this book to discover the mysteries of Universal Source, how we are guided with love from above to create our most magical and beautiful lives, often allowing us to move past pain and misunderstanding to find the truth of Being!**"

~Sheryl I. Glick

Author of A New Life Awaits: Spirit Guided Insights to Support Global Awakening

Host of radio show Healing From Within www.sherylglick.com

"**What a treat to dig into Kimberly Tobin's first novel The Legacy - a supernatural tale centered on Mina, her mother Sheila, and their unusual relationship. I enjoyed the easy flow of the story and especially liked the way she wove in New Age themes such as healing, intuition and psychic knowing. If you dig books with rich characters, a little bit of woo and a sprinkle of wry humor, check this one out. I think you'll like it.**"
~Lisa Wechtenhiser, Intuitive Guide, Coach, Teacher and All-Around Groovy Chick
www.LisaMW.com